PENGUIN CLASSICS

A STUDY IN SCARLET

SIR ARTHUR CONAN DOYLE was born in Edinburgh in 1859 and died in 1930. Into these years he crowded a variety of activity and creative work that earned him an international reputation and inspired the French to give him the epithet of 'the good giant'. He was educated at Stonyhurst and later studied medicine at Edinburgh University, where he became the surgeon's clerk to Professor Joseph Bell whose diagnostic methods provided the model for the science of deduction perfected by Sherlock Holmes.

He set up as a doctor at Southsea and it was while waiting for patients that he began to write. His growing success as an author enabled him to give up his practice and to turn his attention to other subjects. He was a passionate advocate of many causes, ranging from divorce law reform and a Channel tunnel to the issuing of steel helmets to soldiers and inflatable life jackets to sailors. He also campaigned to prove the innocence of individuals, and was instrumental in the introduction of the Court of Criminal Appeal. He was a volunteer physician in the Boer War and later in life became a convert to spiritualism.

As well as his Sherlock Holmes stories, Conan Doyle wrote a number of other works, including historical romances, such as *The Exploits of Brigadier Gerard* (1896) and *Rodney Stone* (1896). In the science fiction tale *The Lost World* (1912), he created another famous character, Professor Challenger, who appears in several later stories.

Sherlock Holmes first appeared in *A Study in Scarlet* in 1887. The Holmes stories soon attracted such a following that Conan Doyle felt the character overshadowed his other work. In 'The Final Problem' (1893) Conan Doyle killed him off, but was obliged by public demand to restore the detective to life. Despite his ambivalence towards Holmes, he remains the character for which Conan Doyle is best known.

IAIN SINCLAIR was born in Cardiff in 1943, and educated at the London School of Film Technique and Trinity College, Dublin. He has lived and worked in east London since 1967 as a secondhand-bookdealer and small press publisher. His long-term obsession with investigating the London badlands (the excuse for meandering riverine expeditions) began with a book of poems and speculations, *Lud Heat* (1975). His novels *White Chappell Scarlet Tracings* (1987), *Downriver* (1991) and *Radon Daughters* (1994) continued these mythological and psychogeographical preoccupations. His latest book, *Landor's Tower* (2001), is something of a departure, being set largely in Wales and the West Country. *Lights Out for the Territory* (1997), a non-fiction work, revisits many of the tropes of his previous London books. Working with Chris Petit, Sinclair has made a number of films for Channel 4, most recently *Asylum* (2000). He is a regular broadcaster and reviewer.

ED GLINERT was born in Dalston, London, and read Classical Hebrew at Manchester University. He recently edited *The Diary of a Nobody* by George and Weedon Grossmith, and has also annotated the collections of Sherlock Holmes stories, *The Adventures of Sherlock Holmes* and *The Memoirs of Sherlock Holmes*, *The Valley of Fear and Selected Cases* and *The Sign of Four* for Penguin Classics. He is the author of *A Literary Guide to London* (Penguin, 2000) and is currently working on a new guide to London for Penguin.

ARTHUR CONAN DOYLE

A Study in Scarlet

Introduction by IAIN SINCLAIR
Notes by ED GLINERT

PENGUIN BOOKS

PENGUIN BOOKS

Published by the Penguin Group
Penguin Books Ltd, 80 Strand, London WC2R 0RL, England
Penguin Putnam Inc., 375 Hudson Street, New York, New York 10014, USA
Penguin Books Australia Ltd, 250 Camberwell Road, Camberwell, Victoria 3124, Australia
Penguin Books Canada Ltd, 10 Alcorn Avenue, Toronto, Ontario, Canada M4V 3B2
Penguin Books India (P) Ltd, 11 Community Centre, Panchsheel Park, New Delhi – 110 017, India
Penguin Books (NZ) Ltd, Cnr Rosedale and Airborne Roads, Albany, Auckland, New Zealand
Penguin Books (South Africa) (Pty) Ltd, 24 Sturdee Avenue, Rosebank 2196, South Africa

Penguin Books Ltd, Registered Offices: 80 Strand, London WC2R 0RL, England

www.penguin.com

A Study in Scarlet first published 1887
Published in Penguin Classics 2001

024

Introduction copyright © Iain Sinclair, 2001
Notes copyright © Ed Glinert, 2001
All rights reserved

The moral right of the authors of the Introduction and Notes has been asserted

Set in 10/12.5 pt Monotype Baskerville
Typeset by Rowland Phototypesetting Ltd, Bury St Edmunds, Suffolk

Printed and bound in Great Britain by Clays Ltd, Elcograf S.p.A.

ISBN-13: 978-0-14-043908-3

www.greenpenguin.co.uk

CONTENTS

INTRODUCTION*

> All art is at once surface and symbol.
> Those who go beneath the surface do so at their peril.
> Those who read the symbol do so at their peril.
> Oscar Wilde, *The Picture of Dorian Gray*

In the world of fly-by-night publications in gaudy pictorial wrappers, significant events all too frequently pass unnoticed. There is a symbiotic relationship between over-dramatized 'true crime' reportage and transient works of fiction. Without the intervention of an investigator of genius, the murder of a foreigner (the member of an outlandish, polygamous sect) in an 'ill-omened and minatory' house, off the Brixton Road, would seem to belong in the pages of the yellow press. On railway station book racks, shilling shockers are distinguished from the sensational journalism that inspired them only by their price.

In Southsea, a moonlighting oculist with an empty waiting room, a man with time to soak up all the criminous fiction on which he can lay his hands, takes his first shot at penning a lurid shocker. 'The plot thickens,' he writes. 'I began to smell a rat.' He doesn't sweat over this magazine fodder, as he would over one of his serious historical romances. He wraps the business up – hawk-nosed detective and bumbling sidekick, comic Scotland Yard functionaries, a killing on the wrong side of the river, capture of criminal – in a brisk eighty

---

* WARNING: *In discussing this story it has sometimes been unavoidable that crucial elements of the plot have been given away. Readers encountering this story for the first time, therefore, might prefer to read this Introduction afterwards.*

pages. He is then faced with stretching this effective, page-turning short story into a saleable novella. Professional hacks have plenty of tricks with white spaces, breaking the chapter at the top of a nice bare page. But the disappointed medical man was new to the game, so he folded in a Western yarn, padded out with purple landscape passages, melodramatic villains and a lachrymose sentimentality that would have embarrassed John Ford at his most Irish.

The working title, *A Tangled Skein*, was a turkey. But it would have to do, while the putative Edgar Allan Poe niggled at his plot. Ormond Sacker, a retired military surgeon, back from a skirmish on the North-West Frontier, relates the adventures of a consulting detective with a surname borrowed from a Harvard professor of anatomy and physiology, the author of many volumes of popular light verse: Oliver Wendell Holmes. Add a preposterous Christian name and the readership for mystery fiction would be introduced to: Mr Sherrinford Holmes.

The author of this fiasco, according to Michael Dibdin in his first novel (*The Last Sherlock Holmes Story*, 1978 – a pitting of the Victorian detective against Jack the Ripper), was always 'getting the dates wrong, falling over the facts, confusing the names'. Editors, to whom the struggling general practitioner submitted his manuscript, were cautious or unenthusiastic. The novella was turned down by the *Cornhill Magazine*, as well as by publishers Warne and Arrowsmith. Eventually, Ward, Lock & Co. agreed to issue it as part of *Beeton's Christmas Annual* in November 1887. By that time, Arthur Conan Doyle had fixed on a new title, *A Study in Scarlet*, and more considered names for his protagonists: Doctor John H. Watson and Sherlock Holmes. Out of such unpromising beginnings, out of financial necessity, boredom, a hungry perusal of earlier models, emerged a book and a set of characters who were to remain as much a part of the fabric of London as the street in which they lived. Their fictitious address, established in the heritage catalogue, took its place alongside Winston Churchill's wartime command bunker, the Tower of London, and the waxworks of Madame Tussaud.

Holmes and Watson were instant immortals, springing, full-grown and two-thirds formed, from the author's head. They were inevitable, a force of nature. It was impossible to believe that they had not always been there: the same age, the same clothes, the same room. Conan Doyle's language was fated. The pattern of words on the page was, immediately, so familiar that *A Study in Scarlet*, like *Hamlet*, seemed to be a work written entirely in quotations. Conan Doyle was taking down a form of dictation, accessing voices from a parallel universe (where they had always been present). He achieved, at his first attempt, the absolute feat in the creation of character: he wrote himself out. Holmes and Watson are unauthored. There are stories, Watson refers to them, cases that cannot be told: 'The Giant Rat of Sumatra', 'The Adventure of the Sussex Vampire'.

The public understood, they responded in a way that publishers (who inevitably get these things wrong) failed to do. They understood that 'Arthur Conan Doyle' was a front, a smokescreen, the facilitator of these extraordinary adventures. A hierarchy was very soon established: Dr Watson as scribe, Holmes as true author, working his friend like a ventriloquist, amazing and intriguing him – with Conan Doyle as no more than Watson's literary agent. The lowest of the low. A grubber. A man of business.

Publication of *A Study in Scarlet*, one year before the Whitechapel Ripper murders, was an event of some consequence. Conan Doyle had landed himself with a golem, an unwanted champion who would dominate the rest of his life; a creature who couldn't be killed off (despite his plunge, wrapped in the arms of his dark contrary, Professor Moriarty, into the Reichenbach Falls).

If the plotting and construction of *A Study in Scarlet* are undistinguished, the characterization is inspired. The sense of pace and urgency, nervous rushes across a London terrain that was still relatively unknown to the author, coupled with the establishment of a base at 221B Baker Street, was masterly. The damaged narrator who is convalescing, after receiving a 'Jezail bullet' in the shoulder, during the second Afghan campaign, drifts without purpose through the city. 'I naturally gravitated to London, that great cesspool into which all the loungers and idlers of the Empire are irresistibly drained.' Watson, existing on his half-pension, friendless, without connections, is a sunscorched Xerox of one of Oscar Wilde's late-century exquisites. Boredom is a necessary vice, not the caste mark of a superior being. His life is without content. Trapped within a posthumous narrative, a prehistory that is shaky at best (the Afghan wound shifting, as he recalls it in the course of subsequent Sherlockian adventures, from shoulder to leg to Achilles' tendon), Watson is eager to discover and define himself by infiltrating the seductive shadow-world of the consulting detective. The outsider (a provincial like Conan Doyle) is integrated into the complex 'novel' of the metropolis. A 'marriage' is arranged to the benefit of both parties. They are connected and earthed. Holmes, preternaturally gifted, vain, emotionally repressed, finds the one person 'innocent' enough to do justice to his legend. Newspaper accounts of the crimes he has solved will be fraudulent; propaganda bent, then as now, by 'off-the-record' leaks and semi-official briefings.

Pedants, close readers, have twitted Conan Doyle for the way he allows Watson to misread Holmes's character. In *A Study in Scarlet* he draws up – like a lovesick parlour maid – a list of his co-tenant's 'limits'. Under 'Knowledge of Literature', he enters 'Nil'. He is astonished to discover that Holmes has never heard of Carlyle. And yet, a new case launched, Holmes is quoting Carlyle, quoting Goethe; rattling away like a cultural blagger auditioning for a radio talk-slot. It's not that the author is careless with his creations. His creations grow away from him, pick up their own momentum, as their narratives are ghosted by the forms and forces of the city. Watson is an unreliable witness, because he is not in possession of all the facts. He works from a memory-landscape that ages with him; nothing is definitively fixed. All confessions are subject to revision.

What hooks the reader from the first sentence of the first story in which Sherlock Holmes appears is the inevitability of the tale told. Nothing showy, no tricks. Plain language that reads like a medical practitioner's case notes. The narrator announces himself and pre-pares the ground for the introduction of this mysterious other, the loved one; object of fascination, absurdity, excitement. We are pre-sented with a burnt-out case (not yet optioned by Graham Greene). A man, back from the war zone, searching ineffectually for an energy source. Watson is often confused with Conan Doyle: both are sturdy imperialists, bustling, sensible romantics, susceptible to a pretty ankle.

Both require the invention of a Byronic alter ego – narcissistic, theatrical – through which to enact their darker fantasies. Sherlock Holmes erupts into *A Study in Scarlet* with the shock of poetry outraging well-behaved, conservative prose.

Conan Doyle is an impresario of pantomime effects. Watson, having been shifted rapidly across the landscape of London ('private hotel in the Strand', Criterion Bar, lunch at the Holborn, hansom cab), finds himself back at his old hospital, Bart's, in the company of his former dresser, Stamford. Holmes is discovered, through dim, smoky light, busking frantically in the style of Stevenson's Dr Jekyll. Doyle's description is virtually a stage direction: 'This was a lofty chamber, lined and littered with countless bottles. Broad, low tables were scattered about, which bristled with retorts, test-tubes, and little Bunsen lamps with their blue flickering flames. There was only one student in the room, who was bending over a distant table absorbed in his work.'

Every gesture is dramatic, designed to stun. Holmes springs or twists or shouts. 'I've found it! I've found it.' Every utterance comes with self-contained exclamation marks. He'll leap from beating a cadaver with a stick to the discovery of 'an infallible test for blood stains', to crushing Watson's hand in a manly grip. Off-guard, wincing from the pain, the doctor is amazed by Holmes's opening gambit: 'You have been in Afghanistan, I perceive?' Absurdist theatre in its purist form.

No Sherlockian investigator, not one of the imitators, copies or off-cuts, all the way down the line from Austin Freeman's Dr Thorndyke to Sexton Blake, has matched the weird immediacy of the original. Holmes is the classically divided man that the age required: alchemist and rigorous scientific experimenter, furious walker and definitive slacker, athlete and dope fiend. He could, as the mood took him, be Trappist or motormouth. He was at once the anonymous uncoverer of secrets and the egotist who ensures that – through Watson – an approved biography would be scripted and left for posterity. Holmes is forever lurching between incompatible polarities. He tries to ensure his immortality by committing suicide at the height of his fame, and is then persuaded into a comeback. A grand old trouper, he stays on the boards from the age of Henry Irving to the first rattle of Nöel Coward's cocktail-shaker. By the finish, voice is all that's left:

a mellifluous Gielgud whisper offering a series of over-rehearsed and under-remembered anecdotes.

The murder, on the dark side of the Thames, the word *rache* scrawled in blood on the wall of a deserted house, the footprints in the mud; all these tropes, bad weather/sick city, still worked through such films as David Fincher's *Seven*, are conjured by Holmes so that he can demonstrate his astonishing skills. Great detectives contrive their own microclimates. Like quest heroes of old, they invent the crimes that test and prove their claims of omniscience. Without the lowlife iniquities of the Brixton Road, there can be no safe domestic enclosure in Baker Street. Without malignant darkness and yellow fog, there is no fire in the hearth, no soft glow of lamplight. When Holmes is incapacitated by ennui, indulging in his 'seven-per-cent solution', he wills a crime, terrible enough to excite him, out of the ether. A crumpled body in a locked room. A coded message on the table. A league of red-headed men. Then he comes to life and London comes to life with him. Awful though the notion might be, the anguish of an unemployed Holmes (echoed and reinforced by a blocked author who admits that he finds it unendurable to cobble together another plot) is part of a cultural psychosis that finds its resolution in the late century's most brutal sequence of sacrifices, the Jack the Ripper murders. Only after these lurid brutalities can the public be roused from their inertia and made to address the social problems of prostitution, appalling housing conditions, squalor and destitution of the East End.

Holmes affects us so deeply because he is both of his time and out of it, a temporary immortal. *A Study in Scarlet* (1887) was one of a number of popular books, genre fiction, some of it published in wrappers, creating the myths by which the late-Victorian period can still be accessed. These works are prophetic; through them we can see what will happen, what *must* happen. Speculative scenarios run ahead of mundane facts: political and social reality is always second-hand. It has been explored and exploited, road-tested by imaginative authors operating in those zones that are only acknowledged by compendium reviews in the humblest corners of the broadsheets. With the passage of time, the throwaway leaflet, the pulp paperback, acquires a posthumous gravity. When it is too late to do anything about it, we begin to franchise (and misinterpret) the visions of writers like Arthur Machen, William Hope Hodgson, Philip K. Dick, Michael Moorcock and J. G. Ballard.

The key Victorian fictions overlap, shadow each other, until their lead characters achieve an independent existence: they are part of the perpetual dream of the city. Stevenson's *Strange Case of Dr Jekyll and Mr Hyde* (1886), Fergus Hume's *The Mystery of a Hansom Cab* (1886), Oscar Wilde's *The Picture of Dorian Gray* (1890), M. P. Shiel's *Prince Zaleski* (1895), Bram Stoker's *Dracula* (1897), Richard Marsh's *The Beetle* (1897): very different but interconnected tales, pertinent fables for the end of a century. They live on the cusp, between Newton and Einstein. Heavy with nostalgia for that which is passing (the exhilarating panoramas of Dickens and Wilkie Collins), they offer a blasphemous welcome to the age of Freud – when all their subversive delights will be 'explained' and dishonoured.

Wilde and Conan Doyle dined together, when they were courted by a representative of *Lippincott's Magazine*, who successfully commissioned *The Picture of Dorian Gray* and *The Sign of Four*. Wilde expressed his admiration for Conan Doyle's *Micah Clarke*. But Conan Doyle, in his turn, had pre-empted Wilde's languid men about town by setting up Holmes and Watson in their cosy bachelor apartment. 'Nowadays,' Wilde wrote, 'all the married men live like bachelors, and all the bachelors like married men' (*The Picture of Dorian Gray*).

The enfeebled Watson, who admits to 'another set of vices when I'm well', has encountered the dark, mercurial Holmes in the lab at Bart's. His future partner offers shares in his 'diggings': '. . . a couple of comfortable bedrooms and a single large airy sitting-room' on the first floor in Baker Street. Before this lurch into domesticity, and the admission that he would 'prefer having a partner to being alone', Watson's enervated lifestyle would run along quite nicely with Wilde's *fin de siècle* decadence. The fellow dinner guests, Conan Doyle and Wilde, were rehearsing their own forms of urban theatre: Wilde through modulated speeches and artfully staged dialogues; Conan Doyle through melodrama and Grand Guignol shocks, quick-acting poisons, cab chases, Houdini handcuffs, disguises and transvestism.

Dr John Watson, presented in film versions of the legend as a bluff, tweedy, no-nonsense Englishman, a Nigel (Bruce or Stock), doesn't begin that way. He loafs about town, hangs out at the Criterion Bar, picks up 'young Stamford'. He listens, in fascination, to descriptions of Holmes who is, apparently, 'a little queer in his ideas'. Watson, in fact, starts out as if determined to justify his original, deleted moniker: Ormond Sacker (cousin to Leopold von Sacher-Masoch?). Whiling away the hours when Holmes is out in the streets, chasing his prey, Watson idles with a copy of Henri Murger's *Vie de Bohème*.

No. 221B Baker Street is a bohemian ménage. Tobacco kept in Persian slippers, bullet holes in the wall, correspondence transfixed with a dagger, and enough cocaine for a three-hits-a-day habit. (Is this one of the reasons why Holmes sets out to charm and 'seduce' Watson? As a medical man he might have easy access to substances that were not then illicit, but which came with a dubious reputation. Watson was superb cover. A casualty of war on a half-pension. A natural 'straight' who could be persuaded to become scribe and amanuensis to a glittering, nocturnal career. Watson was invented to invent Sherlock Holmes.)

Holmes, sawing away on the violin like something out of the Incredible String Band, is a boho poser, a Huysmans aesthete. His attitude to the lower orders – coppers who have come up through the ranks – is patronizing. A procession of curious folk, emblematic figures representing the theatrical strands of London life, visit Holmes. What, for example, is Watson to make of the 'railway porter in his velveteen uniform'? These hesitant members of an exotic underclass blink into the daylight like the feral witnesses produced at the trial of Oscar Wilde.

Watson is in a relationship with Holmes such as the one to which Wilde alludes in *The Picture of Dorian Gray*: 'More than an acquaintance, less than a friend.' He withdraws to his bedroom, so that Holmes can conduct his interviews in their shared sitting-room. Holmes is like an author, a school-of-Mayhew social analyst, receiving reports of the city: the 'little sallow, rat-faced' policeman, the 'fashionably-dressed' young girl, the 'grey-headed, seedy' fellow who might have been a 'Jew pedlar', the 'slip-shod elderly woman'. Each character flounces on set, trying for a part in one of Conan Doyle's fictions. They fail to tempt Holmes from his room. His self-regard remains unpricked. He waits for the opportunity to amaze his new flatmate, to earn the compliments that would bring the blood to his cheeks. 'My companion flushed up with pleasure at my words,' Watson tells us, 'and the earnest way in which I uttered them. I had already observed that he was as sensitive to flattery on the score of his art as any girl could be of her beauty.'

What Watson (on Conan Doyle's behalf) has to provide is a framework in which Holmes can demonstrate his genius. At first reading – which was, after all, the only reading for which the story was intended – *A Study in Scarlet* works superbly up to the point where the body is discovered in the deserted house, off the Brixton Road. The long American flashback and the abrupt resolution are unconvincing and melodramatic. The tale is assembled with a breathtaking exhibition of generic promiscuity: mystery, shilling shocker, supernatural, Western and romance. Conan Doyle borrows from all the popular forms and achieves something that is his own. He anticipates the age of the comic book superhero: Holmes has his uniform, his eccentricities, his 'cave'. From his privileged retreat (with tame landlady and sidekick), he raids the energy map of the city. He is capable of shape-shifting. He can vanish for weeks at a time – or disappear into Tibet. His identity is elastic. His tricks are electrifying: part Dr Faustus, part Spring-Heel'd Jack. And, as with the multiverse of the comic strip, the Holmes saga exhibits signs of cross-pollination, withdrawals from (or previews of) other archetypal figures and post-literary identities. Giving themselves up to the relativity of the Sherlockian cosmology encourages future Londoners to time-travel, to re-occupy the alleys, highways and suburbs of the past.

From its opening, *A Study in Scarlet*, pared-down and direct, operates like a coded manuscript. It is uniquely itself, but it also seems to be about something else. Laboured interpretations are the retrospective delight of literary snoops and textual pedants. Like characters in an M. R. James story, we slide a volume from the over-burdened shelves and waste hours, trying to make sense of a perfectly innocent engraving. The cover illustration for the *Beeton's Christmas Annual*, featuring *A*

Study in Scarlet, depicts an adept rising from his chair – in terror of some shape in the surrounding darkness – reaching out towards a suspended lamp. It is not clear whether he has just lit the lamp or whether he is about to snuff out the wick. On the table in front of him is a selection of paraphernalia that is as much alchemical as scientific. At his feet is a partly rolled sheet of paper. Chapter 7 of *A Study in Scarlet* is entitled 'Light in the Darkness'.

The elements are magical, covert. Holmes is presented as a sort of conjuror, fiddling with retorts, obsessively pursuing obscure and apparently impractical researches. It is no accident that he is discovered in a laboratory at Bart's in Smithfield: one of the oldest and most mysterious quarters of London, part of a Templar enclave. As Joy Hancox points out in *The Byrom Connection* (1992): 'It is clear that there was an hermetic group in Bartholomew Close based around John Dee's kinsman, David.' She goes on to stress the close connection between experiments in speculative philosophy and the hospital. Holmes, the fictitious consulting detective, an appropriate figure for his era, is in a line of descent from the much-mythologized Elizabethan magus, Dr John Dee.

Alchemy depends upon twin powders, the scarlet and the white. And these are the motifs that Conan Doyle stresses: paper and blood, a sanguinary message scrawled on damp plaster. *A Study in Scarlet* becomes a literal scarlet study, the cell of an alchemist. R. Austin Freeman who, in Dr Thorndyke, created one of the most credible successors to Sherlock Holmes, published the first Thorndyke adventure as *The Red Thumb Mark*.

'Red', according to Peter Ackroyd (in *London: The Biography*, 2000), 'is London's colour.' G. K. Chesterton, in *The Napoleon of Notting Hill* (1904), writes that 'The colour is everywhere, even in the ground of the city itself: the bright red layers of oxidized iron in the London clay identified conflagrations which took place almost two thousand years ago.' Conan Doyle's title, his 'study in scarlet', is more than Gothic scene-setting, it identifies the novel as growing from the topography of London – and belonging to a secret tradition. 'No red-headed clients to vex us with their conundrums.'

When I wrote my first novel, which was in part an investigation of unsolved crimes from the late Victorian period, I read and re-read all the Sherlock Holmes stories. *A Study in Scarlet*, the more I tried to understand its peculiar fascination, struck me as having a twofold nature: first, the unhesitating conviction of a language-window, or hinge, through which it was possible to enter the London of the 1880s – and then, more disturbingly, as you accepted the author's invitation and gave yourself up to that world, the realization that the order of words, the names chosen, was prophetic. The first Sherlock Holmes story is a device by which coming events are foretold. I found, even though I had my title before I started to work my way through Conan Doyle, that I was echoing the master: *White Chappell, Scarlet Tracings*.

Had Conan Doyle, in the trance of composition, achieved a pre-vision of the Ripper murders and published them a year ahead of the event? I was indulging a common fantasy. Many writers had taken the obvious step of pitting those mythical contraries, the great fictional detective and the infamous Whitechapel butcher, against each other. Michael Dibdin in *The Last Sherlock Holmes Story* (1978) and Ellery Queen with *A Study in Terror* (1966) were distinguished examples of the genre. Other versions include *The Mycroft Memoranda* (1984) by Ray Walsh and *Sherlock Holmes and Jack the Ripper* (1953) by Gordon Neitzke. John Sladek's *Black Aura* (1974) proposed Doctor Watson as a Ripper suspect.

'In solving a problem of this sort,' said Holmes, 'the grand thing is to be able to go backwards.' And so I believed. The frequently re-issued pages of print that make up any collected edition, or Book Club edition, of *A Study in Scarlet* would do. I treated Conan Doyle's prose as the artist Tom Phillips treated his *A Humument* (1980) project (the doctoring of W. H. Mallock's Victorian novel, *A Human Document*, 1892); I blacked out words until I achieved a sort of planchette message (appropriate to Conan Doyle's later interest in spiritualism and communication with the dead).

Soon the first page of *A Study in Scarlet* looked as if it had been savaged by a prison censor. Strange new phrases were revealed: 'I took my Doctor and Netley through the course prescribed for surgeons ... struck the shoulder ... shattered the bone and grazed the sub-clavian artery ... fallen into the hands of the murderous ... removed to the base hospital.' Here, in my perverse reading, were the key elements of the Ripper crimes as fabled by Joseph Sickert, son of the painter, and franchised by Stephen Knight in his book, *The Final Solution* (1976). The royal surgeon, Sir William Withey Gull, and his coachman, John Netley, are launched on their terrible quest. The warning has been made, coded into this populist yarn, a year or so ahead of itself. Life, by this reading, is merely the confirmation of the best fiction.

My connection of Gull, a successful society surgeon and Freemason, with the fiercely agnostic (and unclubbable) Holmes might seem forced; but the morphic resonance is undoubtedly there. In *The World of Sherlock Holmes* (1973), Michael Harrison writes: 'What Sir William Gull had become to the Royal Family . . . Sherlock Holmes – even by the mid-'Eighties – was well on the way to becoming in the field of protecting the Great from their enemies' malice.' Precisely the act for which Gull fell under suspicion in the case of the Ripper murders.

Using the names of characters to signal hidden qualities has always been a favourite trick for authors. We look with interest therefore at Conan Doyle's 'Mason of Bradford' as a back-reference to a conspiratorial theme. The name of the marginal, but important, figure who introduces Holmes to Watson is 'young Stamford' – which was the town, lightly disguised, where my renegade posse of bookdealers find their own grail, the true first edition, in book form, of *A Study in Scarlet*: the legendary variant that preceded the appearance in *Beeton's Christmas Annual*. This item, according to the bibliographer, Gaby Goldscheider, is 'a book so scarce that it has yet to be located' (1977).

Conan Doyle, disturbed by his own 'bad' father, Charles Doyle, a failed artist, a mentally unstable drunk, leaves echoes in *A Study in Scarlet* of a thwarted man, revenging himself by scrawling *rache* on the wall with a long fingernail. The name of the second victim, stabbed by Jefferson Hope, is Stangerson (with its anagrammatic echoes of 'stranger son'). And there are more orphans, lost sons, among the index of personnel: the Scotland Yard detective Greg*son* and, crucially, the rechristened Wat*son* (what son?). Knowingly or unknowingly, Conan Doyle's naming of characters had a ludic aspect. 'Greg', according to Jonathon Green's *Dictionary of Slang* (1998), is an Irish colloquialism for 'tease'. Conan Doyle had Irish blood on both sides of his ancestry.

If my insistence on a system of subliminal coding is a way of 'legitimatizing' the enduring fascination of this awkwardly structured example of late nineteenth-century genre fiction, it is a minor element in what becomes an enduring and evocative way of reading Victorian London. Conan Doyle realizes, right at the start, that his subject is energy, volition: the survival of individual consciousness against the crushing entropy of the city. London was still, just, knowable. Holmes, like a psychogeographer, disappears into the map. Crime is the motivation, the motor force that gets him up from his chair. Unlike his Parisian contemporaries, he is no *flâneur*: he is a purposeful stalker. 'The game's afoot.' Reach for the Bradshaw. Summon a hansom and off into the purlieus, the ominously unvoiced suburbs.

With the idea of stalking, we come on a motif that is very important to Conan Doyle (and to the mythology of London), the figure of the dog – the urban precursor of the hellish beast of Dartmoor, the Baskerville hound. The dog that didn't bark (from 'Silver Blaze') is one of Conan Doyle's best-known effects. Less has been heard of Dr Watson's invisible bull pup. The keeping of this animal is 'confessed' when Watson lists his drawbacks, before he moves in with Holmes. But the phantom beast is never heard from again. His abrupt disappearance is compensated for in a plethora of canine imagery. 'The old hound is best.' 'I am one of the hounds not the wolf.' Holmes, 'coming upon the right scent', is frequently described in metaphors taken from the hunting field. 'I would dog them and follow them.' 'Gregson, Lestrade, and Holmes sprang upon him like so many staghounds.'

'Supposing one man wished to dog another through London?' That question frames the entire Sherlockian project. Every story is a chain of watchers and reporters: Conan Doyle ghosting Watson, Watson inventing Holmes, Holmes trying to become the personification of the city's ambiguities and excesses. Insults and oaths have a canine colouring: 'You hound!' Or: 'You dog! I have hunted you from Salt Lake City to St Petersburg.' Or: 'Who talks of murdering a mad dog?'

One of the most outlandish episodes in *A Study in Scarlet* is the killing of the dog. Holmes proves his poison-pill thesis by dosing the landlady's conveniently sick terrier. He waits impatiently for results. Nothing happens and he realizes (or hopes) that the animal has been given a placebo. His relief is considerable when the dog obligingly keels over: '. . . it gave a convulsive shiver in every limb, and lay as rigid and lifeless as if it had been struck by lightning.'

A troubling cameo, but Holmes warns us off. 'It is a mistake,' he says, 'to confound strangeness with mystery.' Established in his Baker Street set, the consulting detective is ready to deal with whatever mysteries London can invent to confound and charm him. 'Sometimes he spent his day at the chemical laboratory, sometimes in the dissecting-rooms, and occasionally in long walks, which appeared to take him into the lowest portions of the city.' Holmes was shadowing Rimbaud and Verlaine as they detoured and rambled through Limehouse and around the newly dug deepwater docks, brooding on future voyages. With his sense of theatre, his eccentric studies, his urban peregrinations, Holmes is the perfect model for the metropolitan poet, the psychogeographer. Watson is pure prose, functional, unfussy – but not quite as dim as he presents himself. The convalescent military surgeon comes, by steady increments, to appreciate the city. It is revealed to him through his travels with Holmes; glimpses from the window of a hansom cab racing towards the site of the latest atrocity. 'We did indeed get a fleeting view of a stretch of the Thames, with the lamps shining upon the broad, silent water; but our cab dashed on, and was soon involved in a labyrinth of streets upon the other side.'

The twinned-quest heroes, knight and squire, journey between the familiar clutter of their Baker Street den and the dark wilderness of the city, with its mazy lanes and secret rooms; between memory and forgetfulness, life and death. As they jolt over the cobbles, Holmes recites a litany of place names: 'Wandsworth Road. Priory Road. Larkhill Lane. Stockwell Place. Robert Street. Coldharbour Lane.' Watson, as Conan Doyle's representative, is initiated into the mysteries of place. The particulars of London with its 'mud-coloured clouds' and its 'endless procession of faces' become a phantasmagoric lantern show of all that is still to be written; 'real life' criminals (the poisoner Neill Cream arriving, like one of Conan Doyle's avengers, from across the Atlantic, to take up residence in the South London streets featured in *A Study in Scarlet*) and unborn figures of fantasy. 'If he be Mr Hyde, I shall be Mr Seek.' Conan Doyle will have taken to heart those words in his paper-wrappered copy of Stevenson's *Strange Case of Dr Jekyll and Mr Hyde* (1886).

The would-be author indulged in 'voracious and indiscriminate reading' as he waited for the patients who would never arrive in his Southsea surgery. And through his reading, reveries about his time as a medical student in Edinburgh, the inspirational Dr Joseph Bell, there emerged the outline of one of the stories by which the age would be defined. Conan Doyle was conducting a seance with the future, tapping and forcing – until he was forced to rise, like the figure drawn on the cover *Beeton's Christmas Annual*, to reach out towards the suspended lamp, to weave a fable from the shadows on the wall.

FURTHER READING

BIOGRAPHY

Baring-Gould, William S., *Sherlock Holmes, A Biography* (1962)
Harrison, Michael, *The World of Sherlock Holmes* (1973)
Pearsall, Ronald, *Conan Doyle, A Biographical Solution* (1977)
Starrett, Vincent, *The Private Life of Sherlock Holmes* (1933)

DRUGS

Collins, Randall, *The Case of the Philosophers' Ring* (1978)
Tracy, Jack and Berkey, Jim, *Subcutaneously, My Dear Watson* (1978)

SHERLOCK HOLMES AND JACK THE RIPPER

Byron Cover, Arthur, *An East Wind Coming* (1979)
Dibdin, Michael, *The Last Sherlock Holmes Story* (1978)
Frost, Mark, *The List of Seven* (1993)
Hanna, Edward B., *The Whitechapel Horrors: A Sherlock Holmes Novel* (1992)
Mitchelson, Austin, *The Baker Street Irregular* (1994)
Queen, Ellery, *A Study in Terror* (1966)
Roberts, Barry, *Sherlock Holmes and the Royal Flush* (1998)
Soares, Jo, *A Samba For Sherlock* (1997)
Sinclair, Iain, *White Chappell, Scarlet Tracings* (1987)
Sladek, John, *Black Aura* (1974)
Thor, Raymond, *Bloodguilty* (1997)

Trow, M. J., *Lestrade and the Ripper* (1988)

Walker, Fred, *I Love My Work* (1996)

Walsh, Ray, *The Mycroft Memoranda* (1984)

Weverka, Robert (novelization), *Murder by Decree* (1979)

Williamson J. N. and Williamson H. B. (eds), *Illustrious Clients Third Casebook* (1953). Contains: 'Sherlock Holmes and Jack the Ripper' by Gordon Neitzke

A SELECTIVE CULLING OF LATE VICTORIAN LITERATURE

Novels whose plots, settings and principal characters continue to haunt the psychic biosphere of London.

It is my contention that certain books, overlapping in theme, leave us with characters who achieve an extra-literary existence. Fictional heroes can be as real, or more real, than the landscape that contains them. They survive in the general consciousness far longer than the public figures who are their mundane contemporaries.

As with the creation of Holmes and Watson (the division of a single being), the notion of splitting and doubling, rational mind and dark unconscious, haunts Victorian fiction. Jekyll and Hyde are an extreme manifestation of the conflict between the domestic and the unrepressed, the William Morris drawing room and the savage alley. 'Man is not truly one, but truly two,' says Dr Jekyll.

In terms of psychogeographic coincidence, it's worth recalling the curious information that Dr Watson supplies in the story 'Black Peter'. Holmes, he tells us, 'had at least five small refuges in different parts of London'. The consulting detective was omnipresent, like a figure of myth. He was, like the fabulous Spring-Heel'd Jack, a fire demon (and revenger) capable of leaping over houses. Holmes's bolt-holes are precisely duplicated by Bram Stoker's Dracula, who deposits nine coffin-loads of Transylvanian earth at a scatter of addresses around London, so that he would always have a convenient burrow in which to disappear. The painter Walter Sickert, a teller of Ripper tales, liked to provide himself with secret studios in obscure parts of the city (a tradition followed by the likes of Lucian Freud and Francis Bacon).

Sometimes a seemingly undistinguished work of popular fiction achieves a success that defies rational explanation. The most ephemeral productions can act as harbingers of future horror. Fergus Hume's *The Mystery of a Hansom Cab* seems to introduce on to the late Victorian set the vehicle in which Dr William Gull (a being both actual and archetypal) would soon crisscross the town on his bloody missions.

Hume, Fergus, *The Mystery of a Hansom Cab* (1886)

James, Henry, *The Turn of the Screw* (1898)

Machen, Arthur, *The Great God Pan and the Inmost Light* (1894)

Marsh, Richard, *The Beetle* (1897)

Morrison, Arthur, *Tales of Mean Streets* (1894)

— *Martin Hewitt, Investigator* (1894)

— *Chronicles of Martin Hewitt* (1895)

Rimbaud, Arthur, *Les Illuminations* (1886)

Shiel, M. P., *Prince Zaleski* (1895)

Stevenson, R. L., *Strange Case of Dr Jekyll and Mr Hyde* (1886)

— *The Suicide Club* (1894)

Stoker, Bram, *Dracula* (1897)

Wells, H. G., *The Time Machine* (1895)

— *The Invisible Man* (1897)

Wilde, Oscar, *The Picture of Dorian Gray* (1890)

CHRONOLOGY

A chronology of Arthur Conan Doyle's life and work is likely to be skeletal. As a highly professional writer, a medical specialist, a public campaigner against injustice, a would-be politician, as well as a sportsman, spiritualist, and well-meaning amateur in fields ranging from skiing to weaponry, he threw himself with generous energy into a variety of lives, any one of which would have satisfied most people. A brief account of his activities can, at best, only suggest the range of an extraordinary life.

1859	Arthur Conan Doyle born at 11 Picardy Place, Edinburgh, on 22 May, second of ten children of Charles Doyle, a civil servant, and Mary Doyle, née Foley. (This year also saw the publication of Darwin's *The Origin of Species*.)
1868–70	Spends two years at Hodder Preparatory School, Lancashire.
1870–75	Spends five years in secondary education at Stonyhurst, the leading Jesuit school, in Lancashire.
1875–6	Attends Jesuit college at Feldkirch, Austria.
1876	Enters Edinburgh University to study medicine. Taught by Joseph Bell, a surgeon at the Edinburgh Infirmary, on whom he later bases some of Sherlock Holmes's powers of detection.
1878	Begins first job, assisting a Dr Richardson in Sheffield. Stays with relatives in Maida Vale, London, his first visit to the capital. Writes novel, *The Narrative of John Smith*, which is lost in the post and never recovered. Works as

assistant in doctor's practice in Ruyton-of-the-eleven-towns, Shropshire, and then in Birmingham.

1879 Publication of first story, 'The Mystery of Sasassa Valley', in the Edinburgh weekly *Chambers's Journal* (September).

1880 Serves as ship's doctor on Greenland whaler the *Hope*.

1881 Serves as ship's doctor on West African cargo steamer the *Mayumba*. Graduates from Edinburgh as Bachelor of Medicine.

1882–90 Establishes solo general medical practice in Southsea, a suburb of Portsmouth, after a brief and unsuccessful partnership with Dr George Turnavine Budd in Plymouth (1882).

1884 Publication in the *Cornhill* magazine of 'J. Habakuk Jephson's Statement', widely taken as a true explanation of the mystery of the *Marie Celeste*.

1885 Marries Louise Hawkins. Obtains a doctorate from Edinburgh for dissertation on syphilis.

1886 Writes *A Study in Scarlet*, the first Sherlock Holmes story, which is rejected by the *Cornhill* magazine and the publishers Arrowsmith but is accepted by Ward Lock who hold it over for a year before publishing.

1887 *A Study in Scarlet* is published in *Beeton's Christmas Annual*.

1889 Birth of first child, Mary Louise. *Micah Clarke*, Conan Doyle's first historical novel, is published. At a meeting arranged by the magazine publishers Lippincott, Conan Doyle is commissioned to write what becomes *The Sign of Four*, the second Sherlock Holmes story.

1890 Publication of *The Firm of Girdlestone*. *The Sign of Four* published in *Lippincott's* magazine. Leaves for Austria to study ophthalmology in Vienna.

1891 Opens short-lived oculist practice in Marylebone, London, half a mile east of Baker Street. First six Holmes short stories published in the *Strand* magazine. Abandons medical career and moves to Norwood, south-east London, to take up writing full time. Publication of *The White Company*.

1892   Birth of Kingsley Conan Doyle. *The Adventures of Sherlock Holmes* collection of short stories published.

1893   Louise diagnosed with tuberculosis. More Sherlock Holmes short stories published in the *Strand* and later collected as *The Memoirs of Sherlock Holmes*. In one of these, 'The Final Problem', Conan Doyle apparently kills off Holmes at the Reichenbach Falls. His father, Charles Doyle, dies in the same year. *The Refugees* published.

1894   Makes a very successful US lecture tour with his brother Innes. Publication of *Round the Red Lamp*, a collection of medical stories.

1896   Publication of *The Exploits of Brigadier Gerard* and *Rodney Stone*. *The Field Bazaar*, a Conan Doyle Holmes pastiche and the first new Holmes work since the detective's 'death', is published in an Edinburgh University student magazine. Moves to Hindhead, Surrey.

1897   Publication of *Uncle Bernac*. Meets and falls in love with Jean Leckie.

1898   Publication of *The Tragedy of the Korosko* and *Songs of Action*.

1900   Serves as a volunteer doctor in South Africa during the Boer War and produces an account of the struggle in *The Great Boer War*. Stands (unsuccessfully) as Liberal Unionist candidate for Edinburgh constituency.

1901   *The Hound of the Baskervilles*, set before Holmes's 'official' death in 'The Final Problem', begins publication in the *Strand*.

1902   Receives knighthood. *The Hound of the Baskervilles* published in book form.

1903   Publication of *The Adventures of Gerard*. Holmes properly resurrected in 'The Empty House', published in the *Strand*.

1905   *The Return of Sherlock Holmes*, the latest collection of Holmes short stories that began with 'The Empty House', published in book form.

1906   Stands (unsuccessfully) as Unionist candidate for Hawick on the Scottish Borders. Publication of *Sir Nigel*. Death of Louise Conan Doyle.

1907 Marries Jean Leckie. Publication of *Through the Magic Door*.

1908 Publication of *Round the Fire Stories*. Moves to Crowborough, Sussex. A new Holmes short story, 'The Singular Experience of Mr John Scott Eccles', later renamed 'The Adventure of Wisteria Lodge', published in the *Strand*.

1909 Joins with journalist E. D. Morel (model for Ned Malone in *The Lost World*) to campaign against brutality of the Belgian Congo regime, and writes *The Crime of the Congo*. Birth of son Denis.

1910 Birth of Adrian. Holmes play, *The Speckled Band*, opens at the Adelphi, London. Holmes short story 'The Devil's Foot' published in the *Strand*.

1911 Holmes short stories 'The Red Circle' and 'The Disappearance of Lady Frances Carfax' published in the *Strand*. Conan Doyle is converted to Irish Home Rule by Sir Roger Casement.

1912 *The Lost World*, now the most famous of Doyle's non-Holmes stories, begins serialization in the *Strand* and is published in book form in October. Birth of Jean.

1913 Publication of *The Poison Belt*. Holmes short story 'The Dying Detective' published in the *Strand*.

1914 Conan Doyle forms volunteer force on outbreak of the First World War. Holmes story *The Valley of Fear* begins serialization in the *Strand*.

1915 Publication of *The Valley of Fear* in book form.

1916 Conan Doyle makes first of several visits to the front line areas and produces an account of the British campaign in France. Joins unsuccessful movement to reprieve Irish patriot Sir Roger Casement from execution for treason following the Easter Rising in Dublin (Lord John Roxton in *The Lost World* is partly based on Casement).

1917 'His Last Bow', subtitled 'The War Service of Sherlock Holmes', published in the *Strand*. The recent Holmes short stories collected as *His Last Bow* and published in book form.

1918 Death of eldest son Kingsley from pneumonia after being wounded at the Somme. Conan Doyle publishes his first book on spiritualism, *The New Revelation*; begins new career as an ardent global campaigner for spiritualism.

1919   Death of younger brother Innes from pneumonia.

1921–7   New Holmes short stories published in the *Strand*.

1921   Death of Conan Doyle's mother, Mary Foley.

1924   Autobiography, *Memories and Adventures*, published.

1926   Publication of third Professor Challenger story, *The Land of Mist* (narrative with a spiritualist theme).

1927   Recent short stories collected in book form as *The Case book of Sherlock Holmes*, the last volume of Holmes stories published.

1929   Appearance of the final Professor Challenger story, 'When the World Screamed', in *The Maracot Deep and Other Stories*.

1930   Arthur Conan Doyle dies on 7 July at home in Crowborough.

A Study in Scarlet

CONTENTS

PART ONE

*Being a reprint from
the reminiscences of John H. Watson MD,
late of the Army Medical Department*

I

Mr Sherlock Holmes

In the year 1878 I took my degree of Doctor of Medicine[1] of the University of London,[2] and proceeded to Netley[3] to go through the course prescribed for surgeons in the army. Having completed my studies there, I was duly attached to the Fifth Northumberland Fusiliers[4] as Assistant Surgeon. The regiment was stationed in India at the time, and before I could join it, the second Afghan war[5] had broken out. On landing at Bombay, I learned that my corps had advanced through the passes, and was already deep in the enemy's country. I followed, however, with many other officers who were in the same situation as myself, and succeeded in reaching Candahar[6] in safety, where I found my regiment, and at once entered upon my new duties.

The campaign brought honours and promotion to many,[7] but for me it had nothing but misfortune and disaster. I was removed from my brigade and attached to the Berkshires,[8] with whom I served at the fatal battle of Maiwand.[9] There I was struck on the shoulder by a Jezail bullet,[10] which shattered the bone and grazed the subclavian artery.[11] I should have fallen into the hands of the murderous Ghazis[12] had it not been for the devotion and courage shown by Murray, my orderly, who threw me across a pack-horse, and succeeded in bringing me safely to the British lines.[13]

Worn with pain, and weak from the prolonged hardships which I had undergone, I was removed, with a great train of wounded sufferers, to the base hospital at Peshawar.[14] Here I rallied, and had already improved so far as to be able to walk about the wards, and even to bask a little upon the verandah, when I was struck down by enteric fever, that curse of our Indian possessions. For months my life was despaired of, and when at last I came to myself and became convalescent, I was so weak and emaciated that a medical board determined that not a day should be lost in sending me back to England. I was dispatched accordingly in the troopship *Orontes*,[15] and landed a month later on Portsmouth jetty, with my health irretrievably ruined, but with permission from a paternal government to spend the next nine months in attempting to improve it.

I had neither kith nor kin in England, and was therefore as free as air – or as free as an income of eleven shillings and sixpence a day will permit a man to be.[16] Under such circumstances I naturally gravitated to London, that great cesspool into which all the loungers and idlers of the Empire are irresistibly drained. There I stayed for some time at a private hotel in the Strand, leading a comfortless, meaningless existence, and spending such money as I had, considerably more freely than I ought. So alarming did the state of my finances become that I soon realized that I must either leave the metropolis and rusticate somewhere in the country, or that I must make a complete alteration in my style of living. Choosing the latter alternative, I began by making up my mind to leave the hotel, and to take up my quarters in some less pretentious and less expensive domicile.

On the very day that I had come to this conclusion, I was standing at the Criterion Bar,[17] when someone tapped me on the shoulder, and turning round I recognized young Stamford, who had been a dresser under me at Bart's.[18] The sight of a friendly face in the great wilderness of London is a pleasant thing indeed to a lonely man. In old days Stamford had never been a particular crony of mine, but now I hailed him with enthusiasm, and he, in his turn, appeared to be delighted to see me. In the exuberance of my joy, I asked him to lunch with me at the Holborn,[19] and we started off together in a hansom.[20]

'Whatever have you been doing with yourself, Watson?' he asked in undisguised wonder, as we rattled through the crowded London streets. 'You are as thin as a lath and as brown as a nut.'

I gave him a short sketch of my adventures, and had hardly concluded it by the time that we reached our destination.

'Poor devil!' he said, commiseratingly, after he had listened to my misfortunes. 'What are you up to now?'

'Looking for lodgings,' I answered. 'Trying to solve the problem as to whether it is possible to get comfortable rooms at a reasonable price.'

'That's a strange thing,' remarked my companion, 'you are the second man today that has used that expression to me.'

'And who was the first?' I asked.

'A fellow who is working at the chemical laboratory up at the hospital. He was bemoaning himself this morning because he could not get someone to go halves with him in some nice rooms which he had found, and which were too much for his purse.'

'By Jove!' I cried; 'if he really wants someone to share the rooms and the expense, I am the very man for him. I should prefer having a partner to being alone.'

Young Stamford looked rather strangely at me over his wineglass. 'You don't know Sherlock Holmes yet,' he said; 'perhaps you would not care for him as a constant companion.'

'Why, what is there against him?'

'Oh, I didn't say there was anything against him. He is a little queer in his ideas – an enthusiast in some branches of science. As far as I know he is a decent fellow enough.'

'A medical student, I suppose?' said I.

'No – I have no idea what he intends to go in for. I believe he is well up in anatomy, and he is a first-class chemist; but, as far as I know, he has never taken out any systematic medical classes. His studies are very desultory and eccentric, but he has amassed a lot of out-of-the-way knowledge which would astonish his professors.'

'Did you never ask him what he was going in for?' I asked.

'No; he is not a man that it is easy to draw out, though he can be communicative enough when the fancy seizes him.'

'I should like to meet him,' I said. 'If I am to lodge with anyone, I should prefer a man of studious and quiet habits. I am not strong enough yet to stand much noise or excitement. I had enough of both in Afghanistan to last me for the remainder of my natural existence. How could I meet this friend of yours?'

'He is sure to be at the laboratory,' returned my companion. 'He either avoids the place for weeks, or else he works there from morning till night. If you like, we will drive round together after luncheon.'

'Certainly,' I answered, and the conversation drifted away into other channels.

As we made our way to the hospital after leaving the Holborn, Stamford gave me a few more particulars about the gentleman whom I proposed to take as a fellow-lodger.

'You mustn't blame me if you don't get on with him,' he said; 'I know nothing more of him than I have learned from meeting him occasionally in the laboratory. You proposed this arrangement, so you must not hold me responsible.'

'If we don't get on it will be easy to part company,' I answered. 'It seems to me, Stamford,' I added, looking hard at my companion, 'that you have some reason for washing your hands of the matter. Is this fellow's temper so formidable, or what is it? Don't be mealy-mouthed about it.'

'It is not easy to express the inexpressible,' he answered with a laugh. 'Holmes is a little too scientific for my tastes – it approaches to cold-bloodedness. I could imagine his giving a friend a little pinch of the latest vegetable alkaloid,[21] not out of malevolence, you understand, but simply out of a spirit of inquiry in order to have an accurate idea of the effects. To do him justice, I think that he would take it himself with the same readiness. He appears to have a passion for definite and exact knowledge.'

'Very right too.'

'Yes, but it may be pushed to excess. When it comes to beating the subjects in the dissecting-rooms with a stick,[22] it is certainly taking rather a bizarre shape.'

'Beating the subjects!'

'Yes, to verify how far bruises may be produced after death. I saw him at it with my own eyes.'

'And yet you say he is not a medical student?'

'No. Heaven knows what the objects of his studies are. But here we are, and you must form your own impressions about him.' As he spoke, we turned down a narrow lane and passed through a small side-door which opened into a wing of the great hospital. It was familiar ground to me, and I needed no guiding as we ascended the bleak stone staircase and made our way down the long corridor with its vista of whitewashed wall and dun-coloured doors. Near the farther end a low arched passage branched away from it and led to the chemical laboratory.

This was a lofty chamber, lined and littered with countless bottles. Broad, low tables were scattered about, which bristled with retorts, test-tubes, and little Bunsen lamps[23] with their blue flickering flames. There was only one student in the room, who was bending over a distant table absorbed in his work. At the sound of our steps he glanced round and sprang to his feet with a cry of pleasure. 'I've found it! I've found it,' he shouted to my companion, running towards us with a test-tube in his hand. 'I have found a re-agent which is precipitated by haemoglobin, and by nothing else.' Had he discovered a gold mine, greater delight could not have shone upon his features.

'Dr Watson, Mr Sherlock Holmes,' said Stamford, introducing us.

'How are you?' he said cordially, gripping my hand with a strength for which I should hardly have given him credit. 'You have been in Afghanistan, I perceive.'[24]

'How on earth did you know that?' I asked in astonishment.

'Never mind,' said he, chuckling to himself. 'The question now is about haemoglobin. No doubt you see the significance of this discovery of mine?'

'It is interesting, chemically, no doubt,' I answered, 'but practically –'

'Why, man, it is the most practical medico-legal discovery for years. Don't you see that it gives us an infallible test for blood stains. Come over here now!' He seized me by the coat-sleeve in his eagerness, and drew me over to the table at which he had been working. 'Let us have some fresh blood,' he said, digging a long bodkin into his finger, and drawing off the resulting drop of blood in a chemical pipette. 'Now, I add this small quantity of blood to a litre of water. You perceive that the resulting mixture has the appearance of pure water. The proportion of blood cannot be more than one in a million. I have no doubt, however, that we shall be able to obtain the characteristic reaction.' As he spoke, he threw into the vessel a few white crystals, and then added some drops of a transparent fluid. In an instant the contents assumed a dull mahogany colour, and a brownish dust was precipitated to the bottom of the glass jar.

'Ha! ha!' he cried, clapping his hands, and looking as delighted as a child with a new toy. 'What do you think of that?'

'It seems to be a very delicate test,' I remarked.

'Beautiful! beautiful! The old guaiacum test[25] was very clumsy and uncertain. So is the microscopic examination for blood corpuscles. The latter is valueless if the stains are a few hours old. Now, this appears to act as well whether the blood is old or new. Had this test been invented, there are hundreds of men now walking the earth who would long ago have paid the penalty of their crimes.'

'Indeed!' I murmured.

'Criminal cases are continually hinging upon that one point. A man is suspected of a crime months perhaps after it has been committed. His linen or clothes are examined and brownish stains discovered upon them. Are they blood stains, or mud stains, or rust stains, or fruit stains, or what are they? That is a question which has puzzled many an expert, and why? Because there was no reliable test. Now we have the Sherlock Holmes test,[26] and there will no longer be any difficulty.'

His eyes fairly glittered as he spoke, and he put his hand over his heart and bowed as if to some applauding crowd conjured up by his imagination.

'You are to be congratulated,' I remarked, considerably surprised at his enthusiasm.

'There was the case of Von Bischoff at Frankfort last year. He would certainly have been hung had this test been in existence. Then there was Mason of Bradford, and the notorious Muller,[27] and Lefevre of Montpellier, and Samson of New Orleans. I could name a score of cases in which it would have been decisive.'

'You seem to be a walking calendar of crime,' said Stamford with a laugh. 'You might start a paper on those lines. Call it the "Police News of the Past".'

'Very interesting reading it might be made, too,' remarked Sherlock Holmes, sticking a small piece of plaster over the prick on his finger. 'I have to be careful,' he continued, turning to me with a smile, 'for I dabble with poisons a good deal.' He held out his hand as he spoke, and I noticed that it was all mottled over with similar pieces of plaster, and discoloured with strong acids.

'We came here on business,' said Stamford, sitting down on a high three-legged stool, and pushing another one in my direction with his foot. 'My friend here wants to take diggings; and as you were complaining that you could get no one to go halves with you, I thought that I had better bring you together.'

Sherlock Holmes seemed delighted at the idea of sharing his rooms with me. 'I have my eye on a suite in Baker Street,' he said, 'which would suit us down to the ground. You don't mind the smell of strong tobacco, I hope?'

'I always smoke "ship's" myself,' I answered.

'That's good enough. I generally have chemicals about, and occasionally do experiments. Would that annoy you?'

'By no means.'

'Let me see – what are my other shortcomings. I get in the dumps at times, and don't open my mouth for days on end. You must not think I am sulky when I do that. Just let me alone, and I'll soon be right. What have you to confess now? It's just as well for two fellows to know the worst of one another before they begin to live together.'

I laughed at this cross-examination. 'I keep a bull pup,'[28] I said, 'and I object to rows because my nerves are shaken, and I get up at all sorts of ungodly hours, and I am extremely lazy. I have another set of vices when I'm well, but those are the principal ones at present.'

'Do you include violin playing in your category of rows?' he asked, anxiously.

'It depends on the player,' I answered. 'A well-played violin is a treat for the gods – a badly-played one –'

'Oh, that's all right,' he cried, with a merry laugh. 'I think we may consider the thing as settled – that is, if the rooms are agreeable to you.'

'When shall we see them?'

'Call for me here at noon tomorrow, and we'll go together and settle everything,' he answered.

'All right – noon exactly,' said I, shaking his hand.

We left him working among his chemicals, and we walked together towards my hotel.

'By the way,' I asked suddenly, stopping and turning upon Stamford, 'how the deuce did he know that I had come from Afghanistan?'

My companion smiled an enigmatical smile. 'That's just his little peculiarity,' he said. 'A good many people have wanted to know how he finds things out.'

'Oh! a mystery is it?' I cried, rubbing my hands. 'This is very piquant. I am much obliged to you for bringing us together. "The proper study of mankind is man,"[29] you know.'

'You must study him, then,' Stamford said, as he bade me good-bye. 'You'll find him a knotty problem, though. I'll wager he learns more about you than you about him. Good-bye.'

'Good-bye,' I answered, and strolled on to my hotel, considerably interested in my new acquaintance.

2

The Science of Deduction

We met next day as he had arranged, and inspected the rooms at No. 221B, Baker Street,[1] of which he had spoken at our meeting. They consisted of a couple of comfortable bedrooms and a single large airy sitting-room, cheerfully furnished, and illuminated by two broad windows. So desirable in every way were the apartments, and so moderate did the terms seem when divided between us, that the bargain was concluded upon the spot, and we at once entered into possession. That very evening I moved my things round from the hotel, and on the following morning Sherlock Holmes followed me with several boxes and portmanteaux. For a day or two we were busily employed in unpacking and laying out our property to the best advantage. That done, we gradually began to settle down and to accommodate ourselves to our new surroundings.

Holmes was certainly not a difficult man to live with. He was quiet in his ways, and his habits were regular. It was rare for him to be up after ten at night, and he had invariably breakfasted and gone out before I rose in the morning. Sometimes he spent his day at the chemical laboratory, sometimes in the dissecting-rooms, and occasionally in long walks, which appeared to take him into the lowest portions of the city.[2] Nothing could exceed his energy when the working fit was upon him; but now and again a reaction would seize him, and for days on end he would lie upon the sofa in the sitting-room, hardly uttering a word or moving a muscle from morning to night. On these occasions I have noticed such a dreamy, vacant expression in his eyes, that I might have suspected him of being addicted to the use of some narcotic, had not the temperance and cleanliness of his whole life forbidden such a notion.

As the weeks went by, my interest in him and my curiosity as to his aims in life gradually deepened and increased. His very person and appearance[3] were such as to strike the attention of the most casual observer. In height he was rather over six feet, and so excessively lean that he seemed to be considerably taller. His eyes were sharp and piercing, save during those intervals of torpor to which I have alluded; and his thin, hawk-like nose gave his whole expression an air of alertness and decision. His chin, too, had the prominence and squareness which mark the man of determination. His hands were invariably blotted with ink and stained with chemicals, yet he was possessed of extraordinary delicacy of touch, as I frequently had occasion to observe when I watched him manipulating his fragile philosophical instruments.

The reader may set me down as a hopeless busybody, when I confess how much this man stimulated my curiosity, and how often I endeavoured to break through the reticence which he showed on all that concerned himself. Before pronouncing judgement, however, be it remembered how objectless was my life, and how little there was to engage my attention. My health forbade me from venturing out unless the weather was exceptionally genial, and I had no friends who would call upon me and break the monotony of my daily existence. Under these circumstances I eagerly hailed the little mystery which hung around my companion, and spent much of my time in endeavouring to unravel it.

He was not studying medicine. He had himself, in reply to a question, confirmed Stamford's opinion in that point. Neither did he appear to have pursued any course of reading which might fit him for a degree in science or any other recognized portal which would give him an entrance into the learned world. Yet his zeal for certain studies was remarkable, and within eccentric limits his knowledge was so extraordinarily ample and minute that his observations have fairly astounded me. Surely no man would work so hard or attain such precise information unless he had some definite end in view. Desultory readers are seldom remarkable for the exactness of their learning. No man burdens his mind with small matters unless he has some very good reason for doing so.

His ignorance was as remarkable as his knowledge. Of contemporary literature, philosophy and politics he appeared to know next to nothing. Upon my quoting Thomas Carlyle, he inquired in the naïvest way who he might be and what he had done.[4] My surprise reached a climax, however, when I found incidentally that he was ignorant of the Copernican Theory and of the composition of the Solar System.[5] That any civilized human being in this nineteenth century should not be aware that the earth travelled round the sun appeared to be to me such an extraordinary fact that I could hardly realize it.

'You appear to be astonished,' he said, smiling at my expression of surprise. 'Now that I do know it I shall do my best to forget it.'

'To forget it!'

'You see,' he explained, 'I consider that a man's brain originally is like a little empty attic, and you have to stock it with such furniture as you choose. A fool takes in all the lumber of every sort that he comes across,[6] so that the knowledge which might be useful to him gets crowded out, or at best is jumbled up with a lot of other things, so that he has a difficulty in laying his hands upon it. Now the skilful workman is very careful indeed as to what he takes into his brain-attic. He will have nothing but the tools which may help him in doing his work, but of these he has a large assortment, and all in the most perfect order. It is a mistake to think that that little room has elastic walls and can distend to any extent. Depend upon it there comes a time when for every addition of knowledge you forget something that you knew before. It is of the highest importance, therefore, not to have useless facts elbowing out the useful ones.'[7]

'But the Solar System!' I protested.

'What the deuce is it to me?' he interrupted impatiently: 'you say that we go round the sun. If we went round the moon it would not make a penny-worth of difference to me or to my work.'

I was on the point of asking him what that work might be, but something in his manner showed me that the question would be an unwelcome one. I pondered over our short conversation, however, and endeavoured to draw my deductions from it. He said that he would acquire no knowledge which did not bear upon his object. Therefore all the knowledge which he possessed was such as would be useful to him. I enumerated in my own mind all the various points upon which he had shown me that he was exceptionally well-informed. I even took a pencil and jotted them down. I could not help smiling at the document when I had completed it. It ran in this way:

Sherlock Holmes – his limits

1 Knowledge of Literature: Nil.[8]
2 Knowledge of Philosophy: Nil.[9]
3 Knowledge of Astronomy: Nil.[10]
4 Knowledge of Politics: Feeble.[11]
5 Knowledge of Botany: Variable. Well up in belladonna, opium, and poisons generally. Knows nothing of practical gardening.
6 Knowledge of Geology: Practical, but limited. Tells at a glance different soils from each other. After walks has shown me splashes upon his trousers, and told me by their colour and consistence in what part of London he had received them.
7 Knowledge of Chemistry: Profound.
8 Knowledge of Anatomy: Accurate, but unsystematic.
9 Knowledge of Sensational Literature: Immense. He appears to know every detail of every horror perpetrated in the century.
10 Plays the violin well.
11 Is an expert singlestick[12] player, boxer, and swordsman.
12 Has a good practical knowledge of British law.

When I had got so far in my list I threw it into the fire in despair. 'If I can only find what the fellow is driving at by reconciling all these accomplishments, and discovering a calling which needs them all,' I said to myself, 'I may as well give up the attempt at once.'

I see that I have alluded above to his powers upon the violin. These were very remarkable, but as eccentric as all his other accomplishments. That he could play pieces, and difficult pieces, I knew well, because at my request he has played me some of Mendelssohn's Lieder,[13] and other favourites. When left to himself, however, he would seldom produce any music or attempt any recognizing air. Leaning back in his arm-chair of an evening, he would close his eyes and scrape carelessly at the fiddle which was thrown across his knee.

Sometimes the chords were sonorous and melancholy. Occasionally they were fantastic and cheerful. Clearly they reflected the thoughts which possessed him, but whether the music aided those thoughts, or whether the playing was simply the result of a whim or fancy, was more than I could determine. I might have rebelled against these exasperating solos had it not been that he usually terminated them by playing in quick succession a whole series of my favourite airs as a slight compensation for the trial upon my patience.

During the first week or so we had no callers, and I had begun to think that my companion was as friendless a man as I was myself. Presently, however, I found that he had many acquaintances, and those in the most different classes of society. There was one little sallow, rat-faced, dark-eyed fellow, who was introduced to me as Mr Lestrade,[14] and who came three or four times in a single week. One morning a young girl called, fashionably dressed, and stayed for half an hour or more. The same afternoon brought a grey-headed, seedy visitor, looking like a Jew pedlar, who appeared to me to be much excited, and who was closely followed by a slip-shod elderly woman. On another occasion an old white-haired gentleman had an interview with my companion; and on another, a railway porter in his velveteen uniform. When any of these nondescript individuals put in an appearance, Sherlock Holmes used to beg for the use of the sitting-room, and I would retire to my bedroom. He always apologized to me for putting me to this inconvenience. 'I have to use this room as a place of business,' he said, 'and these people are my clients.' Again I had an opportunity of asking him a point-blank question, and again my delicacy prevented me from forcing another man to confide in me. I imagined at the time that he had some strong reason for not alluding to it, but he soon dispelled the idea by coming round to the subject of his accord.

It was upon the 4th of March, as I have good reason to remember, that I rose somewhat earlier than usual, and found that Sherlock Holmes had not yet finished his breakfast. The landlady had become so accustomed to my late habits that my place had not been laid nor my coffee prepared. With the unreasonable petulance of mankind I rang the bell and gave a curt intimation that I was ready. Then I picked up a magazine from the table and attempted to while away the time with it, while my companion munched silently at his toast. One of the articles had a pencil mark at the heading, and I naturally began to run my eye through it.

Its somewhat ambitious title was 'The Book of Life',[15] and it attempted to show how much an observant man might learn by an accurate and systematic examination of all that came in his way. It struck me as being a remarkable mixture of shrewdness and of absurdity. The reasoning was close and intense, but the deductions appeared to me to be far-fetched and exaggerated. The writer claimed by a momentary expression, a twitch of a muscle or a glance of an eye, to fathom a man's inmost thoughts. Deceit, according to him, was an impossibility in the case of one trained to observation and analysis. His conclusions were as infallible as so many propositions of Euclid.[16] So startling would his results appear to the uninitiated that until they learned the processes by which he had arrived at them they might well consider him as a necromancer.

'From a drop of water,' said the writer,

a logician could infer the possibility of an Atlantic or a Niagara without having seen or heard of one or the other. So all life is a great chain, the nature of which is known whenever we are shown a single link of it. Like all other arts, the Science of Deduction and Analysis is one which can only be acquired by long and patient study, nor is life long enough to allow any mortal to attain the highest possible perfection in it. Before turning to these moral and mental aspects of the matter which present the greatest difficulties, let the inquirer begin by mastering more elementary problems. Let him on meeting a fellow-mortal, learn at a glance to distinguish the history of the man, and the trade or profession to which he belongs. Puerile as such an exercise may seem, it sharpens the faculties of observation, and teaches one where to look and what to look for. By a man's finger-nails, by his coat-sleeve, by his boot, by his trouser-knees, by the callosities of his forefinger and thumb, by his expression, by his shirt-cuffs – by each of these things a man's calling is plainly revealed. That all united should fail to enlighten the competent inquirer in any case is almost inconceivable.

'What ineffable twaddle!' I cried, slapping the magazine down on the table; 'I never read such rubbish in my life.'

'What is it?' asked Sherlock Holmes.

'Why, this article,' I said, pointing at it with my egg-spoon as I sat down to my breakfast. 'I see that you have read it since you have marked it. I don't deny that it is smartly written. It irritates me, though. It is evidently the theory of some armchair lounger who evolves all these neat little paradoxes in the seclusion of his own study. It is not practical. I should like to see him clapped down in a third-class carriage on the Underground, and asked to give the trades of all his fellow-travellers. I would lay a thousand to one against him.'

'You would lose your money,' Holmes remarked calmly. 'As for the article, I wrote it myself.'

'You!'

'Yes; I have a turn both for observation and for deduction. The theories which I have expressed there, and which appear to you to be so chimerical, are really extremely practical – so practical that I depend upon them for my bread and cheese.'

'And how!' I asked involuntarily.

'Well, I have a trade of my own. I suppose I am the only one in the world. I'm a consulting detective, if you can understand what that is. Here in London we have lots of Government detectives and lots of private ones. When these fellows are at fault, they come to me, and I manage to put them on the right scent. They lay all the evidence before me, and I am generally able, by the help of my knowledge of the history of crime, to set them straight. There is a strong family resemblance about misdeeds, and if you have all the details of a thousand at your finger ends, it is odd if you can't unravel the thousand and first. Lestrade is a well-known detective. He got himself into a fog recently over a forgery case, and that was what brought him here.'

'And these other people?'

'They are mostly sent on by private inquiry agencies. They are all people who are in trouble about something and want a little enlightenment. I listen to their story, they listen to my comments, and then I pocket my fee.'

'But do you mean to say,' I said, 'that without leaving your room you can unravel some knot which other men can make nothing of, although they have seen every detail for themselves?'

'Quite so. I have a kind of intuition that way. Now and again a case turns up which is a little more complex. Then I have to bustle about and see things with my own eyes. You see I have a lot of special knowledge which I apply to the problem, and which facilitates matters wonderfully. Those rules of deduction laid down in that article which aroused your scorn are invaluable to me in practical work. Observation with me is second nature. You appeared to be surprised when I told you, on our first meeting, that you had come from Afghanistan.'

'You were told, no doubt.'

'Nothing of the sort. I *knew* you came from Afghanistan. From long habit the train of thoughts ran so swiftly through my mind that I arrived at the conclusion without being conscious of intermediate steps. There were such steps, however. The train of reasoning ran: "Here is a gentleman of a medical type, but with the air of a military man. Clearly an army doctor then. He has just come from the tropics, for his face is dark, and that is not the natural tint of his skin, for his wrists are fair. He has undergone hardship and sickness, as his haggard face says clearly. His left arm has been injured. He holds it in a stiff and unnatural manner. Where in the tropics[17] could an English army doctor have seen much hardship and got his arm wounded? Clearly in Afghanistan." The whole train of thought did not occupy a second. I then remarked that you came from Afghanistan, and you were astonished.'

'It is simple enough as you explain it,' I said, smiling. 'You remind me of Edgar Allan Poe's Dupin.[18] I had no idea that such individuals did exist outside of stories.'

Sherlock Holmes rose and lit his pipe. 'No doubt you think that you are complimenting me in comparing me to Dupin,' he observed. 'Now, in my opinion, Dupin was a very inferior fellow.[19] That trick of his of breaking in on his friends' thoughts with an apropos remark after a quarter of an hour's silence is really very showy and superficial. He had some analytical genius, no doubt; but he was by no means such a phenomenon as Poe appeared to imagine.'

'Have you read Gaboriau's works?'[20] I asked. 'Does Lecoq come up to your idea of a detective?'

Sherlock Holmes sniffed sardonically. 'Lecoq was a miserable

bungler,' he said, in an angry voice; 'he had only one thing to rec-
ommend him, and that was his energy. That book made me positively
ill. The question was how to identify an unknown prisoner. I could
have done it in twenty-four hours. Lecoq took six months or so. It
might be made a text-book for detectives to teach them what to avoid.'

I felt rather indignant at having two characters whom I had admired
treated in this cavalier style. I walked over to the window, and stood
looking out into the busy street. 'This fellow may be very clever,' I
said to myself, 'but he is certainly very conceited.'

'There are no crimes and no criminals in these days,' he said,
querulously. 'What is the use of having brains in our profession? I
know well that I have it in me to make my name famous. No man
lives or has ever lived who has brought the same amount of study and
of natural talent to the detection of crime which I have done. And
what is the result? There is no crime to detect, or, at most, some
bungling villainy with a motive so transparent that even a Scotland
Yard[21] official can see through it.'

I was still annoyed at his bumptious style of conversation. I thought
it best to change the topic.

'I wonder what that fellow is looking for?' I asked, pointing to a
stalwart, plainly-dressed individual who was walking slowly down the
other side of the street, looking anxiously at the numbers. He had a
large blue envelope in his hand, and was evidently the bearer of a
message.

'You mean the retired sergeant of Marines,' said Sherlock Holmes.

'Brag and bounce!' thought I to myself. 'He knows that I cannot
verify his guess.'

The thought had hardly passed through my mind when the man
whom we were watching caught sight of the number on our door, and
ran rapidly across the roadway. We heard a loud knock, a deep voice
below, and heavy steps ascending the stair.

'For Mr Sherlock Holmes,' he said, stepping into the room and
handing my friend the letter.

Here was an opportunity of taking the conceit out of him. He little
thought of this when he made that random shot. 'May I ask, my lad,'
I said, in the blandest voice, 'what your trade may be?'

'Commissionaire,[22] sir,' he said, gruffly. 'Uniform away for repairs.'

'And you were?' I asked, with a slightly malicious glance at my companion.

'A sergeant, sir, Royal Marine Light Infantry,[23] sir. No answer? Right, sir.'

He clicked his heels together, raised his hand in a salute, and was gone.

3

The Lauriston Gardens Mystery

I confess that I was considerably startled by this fresh proof of the practical nature of my companion's theories. My respect for his powers of analysis increased wondrously. There still remained some lurking suspicion in my mind, however, that the whole thing was a prearranged episode, intended to dazzle me, though what earthly object he could have in taking me in was past my comprehension. When I looked at him, he had finished reading the note, and his eyes had assumed the vacant, lack-lustre expression which showed mental abstraction.

'How in the world did you deduce that?' I asked.

'Deduce what?' said he, petulantly.

'Why, that he was a retired sergeant of Marines.'

'I have no time for trifles,' he answered brusquely. Then with a smile: 'Excuse my rudeness. You broke the thread of my thoughts; but perhaps it is as well. So you actually were not able to see that that man was a sergeant of Marines?'

'No, indeed.'

'It was easier to know it than to explain why I know it. If you were asked to prove that two and two made four, you might find some difficulty, and yet you are quite sure of the fact. Even across the street I could see a great blue anchor tattooed on the back of the fellow's hand. That smacked of the sea. He had a military carriage, however, and regulation side whiskers. There we have the marine. He was a man with some amount of self-importance and a certain air of command. You must have observed the way in which he held his head and swung his cane. A steady, respectable, middle-aged man, too, on the face of him – all facts which led me to believe that he had been a sergeant.'

'Wonderful!' I ejaculated.

'Commonplace,' said Holmes, though I thought from his expression that he was pleased at my evident surprise and admiration. 'I said just now that there were no criminals. It appears that I am wrong – look at this!' He threw me over the note which the commissionaire had brought.

'Why,' I cried, as I cast my eye over it, 'this is terrible!'

'It does seem to be a little out of the common,' he remarked, calmly. 'Would you mind reading it to me aloud?'[1]

This is the letter which I read to him:

' "My dear Mr Sherlock Holmes, There has been a bad business during the night at 3, Lauriston Gardens,[2] off the Brixton Road. Our man on the beat saw a light there about two in the morning, and as the house was an empty one, suspected that something was amiss. He found the door open, and in the front room, which is bare of furniture, discovered the body of a gentleman, well dressed, and having cards in his pocket bearing the name of 'Enoch J. Drebber, Cleveland, Ohio, U.S.A.' There had been no robbery, nor is there any evidence as to how the man met his death. There are marks of blood in the room, but there is no wound upon his person. We are at a loss as to how he came into the empty house; indeed the whole affair is a puzzler. If you can come round to the house any time before twelve, you will find me there. I have left everything *in statu quo* until I hear from you. If you are unable to come, I shall give you fuller details, and would esteem it a great kindness if you would favour me with your opinion. Yours faithfully, TOBIAS GREGSON." '

'Gregson is the smartest of the Scotland Yarders,' my friend remarked; 'he and Lestrade are the pick of a bad lot. They are both quick and energetic, but conventional – shockingly so. They have their knives into one another, too. They are as jealous as a pair of professional beauties. There will be some fun over this case if they are both put upon the scent.'

I was amazed at the calm way in which he rippled on. 'Surely there is not a moment to be lost,' I cried; 'shall I go and order you a cab?'

'I'm not sure about whether I shall go. I am the most incurably lazy devil that ever stood in shoe leather – that is, when the fit is on me, for I can be spry enough at times.'

'Why, it is just such a chance as you have been longing for.'

'My dear fellow, what does it matter to me? Supposing I unravel the whole matter, you may be sure that Gregson, Lestrade, and Co. will pocket all the credit. That comes of being an unofficial personage.'

'But he begs you to help him.'

'Yes. He knows that I am his superior, and acknowledges it to me; but he would cut his tongue out before he would own it to any third person. However, we may as well go and have a look. I shall work it out on my own hook. I may have a laugh at them, if I have nothing else. Come on!'

He hustled on his overcoat, and bustled about in a way that showed that an energetic fit had superseded the apathetic one.

'Get your hat,' he said.

'You wish me to come?'

'Yes, if you have nothing better to do.' A minute later we were both in a hansom, driving furiously for the Brixton Road.

It was a foggy, cloudy morning, and a dun-coloured veil hung over the house-tops, looking like the reflection of the mud-coloured streets beneath. My companion was in the best of spirits, and prattled away about Cremona fiddles, and the difference between a Stradivarius and an Amati.[3] As for myself, I was silent, for the dull weather and the melancholy business upon which we were engaged, depressed my spirits.

'You don't seem to give much thought to the matter in hand,' I said at last, interrupting Holmes's musical disquisition.

'No data yet,' he answered. 'It is a capital mistake to theorize before you have all the evidence. It biases the judgement.'

'You will have your data soon,' I remarked, pointing with my finger; 'this is the Brixton Road, and that is the house, if I am not very much mistaken.'

'So it is. Stop, driver, stop!' We were still a hundred yards or so from it, but he insisted upon our alighting, and we finished our journey upon foot.

Number 3, Lauriston Gardens, wore an ill-omened and minatory look. It was one of four which stood back some little way from the street, two being occupied and two empty. The latter looked out with three tiers of vacant melancholy windows, which were blank and dreary, save that here and there a 'To Let' card had developed like a cataract upon the bleared panes. A small garden sprinkled over with a scattered eruption of sickly plants separated each of these houses from the street, and was traversed by a narrow pathway, yellowish in colour, and consisting apparently of a mixture of clay and gravel. The whole place was very sloppy from the rain which had fallen through the night. The garden was bounded by a three-foot brick wall with a fringe of wood rails upon the top, and against this wall was leaning a stalwart police constable, surrounded by a small knot of loafers, who craned their necks and strained their eyes in the vain hope of catching some glimpse of the proceedings within.

I had imagined that Sherlock Holmes would at once have hurried into the house and plunged into a study of the mystery. Nothing appeared to be further from his intention. With an air of nonchalance which, under the circumstances, seemed to me to border upon affectation, he lounged up and down the pavement, and gazed vacantly at the ground, the sky, the opposite houses and the line of railings. Having finished his scrutiny, he proceeded slowly down the path, or rather down the fringe of grass which flanked the path, keeping his eyes riveted upon the ground. Twice he stopped and once I saw him smile, and heard him utter an exclamation of satisfaction. There were many marks of footsteps upon the wet clayey soil; but since the police had been coming and going over it, I was unable to see how my companion could hope to learn anything from it. Still, I had had such extraordinary evidence of the quickness of his perceptive faculties, that I had no doubt that he could see a great deal which was hidden from me.

At the door of the house we were met by a tall, white-faced, flaxen-haired man, with a notebook in his hand, who rushed forward and wrung my companion's hand with effusion. 'It is indeed kind of you to come,' he said, 'I have had everything left untouched.'

'Except that!' my friend answered, pointing at the pathway. 'If a herd of buffaloes had passed along there could not be a greater mess. No doubt, however, you had drawn your own conclusions, Gregson, before you permitted this.'

'I have had so much to do inside the house,' the detective said evasively. 'My colleague, Mr Lestrade, is here. I had relied upon him to look after this.'

Holmes glanced at me and raised his eyebrows sardonically. 'With two such men as yourself and Lestrade upon the ground, there will not be much for a third party to find out,' he said.

Gregson rubbed his hands in a self-satisfied way. 'I think we have done all that can be done,' he answered; 'it's a queer case though, and I knew your taste for such things.'

'You did not come here in a cab?'⁴ asked Sherlock Holmes.

'No, sir.'

'Nor Lestrade?'

'No, sir.'

'Then let us go and look at the room.' With which inconsequent remark he strode on into the house, followed by Gregson, whose features expressed his astonishment.

A short passage, bare-planked and dusty, led to the kitchen and offices. Two doors opened out of it to the left and to the right. One of these had obviously been closed for many weeks. The other belonged to the dining-room, which was the apartment in which the mysterious affair had occurred. Holmes walked in, and I followed him with that subdued feeling at my heart which the presence of death inspires.

It was a large square room, looking all the larger from the absence of all furniture. A vulgar flaring paper adorned the walls, but it was blotched in places with mildew, and here and there great strips had become detached and hung down, exposing the yellow plaster beneath. Opposite the door was a showy fireplace, surmounted by a mantelpiece of imitation white marble. On one corner of this was stuck the stump of a red wax candle. The solitary window was so dirty that the light was hazy and uncertain, giving a dull grey tinge to everything, which was intensified by the thick layer of dust which coated the whole apartment.

All these details I observed afterwards. At present my attention was centred upon the single, grim, motionless figure which lay stretched upon the boards, with vacant, sightless eyes staring up at the discoloured ceiling. It was that of a man about forty-three or forty-four years of age, middle-sized, broad-shouldered, with crisp curling black hair, and a short, stubbly beard. He was dressed in a heavy broadcloth frock coat and waistcoat, with light-coloured trousers, and immaculate collar and cuffs. A top hat, well brushed and trim, was placed upon the floor beside him. His hands were clenched and his arms thrown abroad, while his lower limbs were interlocked, as though his death struggle had been a grievous one. On his rigid face there stood an expression of horror, and, as it seemed to me, of hatred, such as I have never seen upon human features. This malignant and terrible contortion, combined with the low forehead, blunt nose, and prognathous jaw, gave the dead man a singularly simious and ape-like appearance, which was increased by his writhing, unnatural posture. I have seen death in many forms, but never has it appeared to me in a more fearsome aspect than in that dark, grimy apartment, which looked out upon one of the main arteries of suburban London.

Lestrade, lean and ferret-like as ever, was standing by the doorway, and greeted my companion and myself.

'This case will make a stir, sir,' he remarked. 'It beats anything I have seen, and I am no chicken.'

'There is no clue?' said Gregson.

'None at all,' chimed in Lestrade.

Sherlock Holmes approached the body, and, kneeling down, examined it intently. 'You are sure that there is no wound?' he asked, pointing to numerous gouts and splashes of blood which lay all round.

'Positive!' cried both detectives.

'Then, of course, this blood belongs to a second individual – presumably the murderer, if murder has been committed. It reminds me of the circumstances attendant on the death of Van Jansen, in Utrecht, in the year '34. Do you remember the case, Gregson?'

'No, Sir.'

'Read it up – you really should. There is nothing new under the sun.[5] It has been done before.'

As he spoke, his nimble fingers were flying here, there, and everywhere, feeling, pressing, unbuttoning, examining, while his eyes wore the same faraway expression which I have already remarked upon. So swiftly was the examination made, that one would hardly have guessed the minuteness with which it was conducted. Finally, he sniffed the dead man's lips, and then glanced at the soles of his patent leather boots.

'He has not been moved at all?' he asked.

'No more than was necessary for the purposes of our examination.'

'You can take him to the mortuary now,' he said. 'There is nothing more to be learned.'

Gregson had a stretcher and four men at hand. At his call they entered the room, and the stranger was lifted and carried out. As they raised him, a ring tinkled down and rolled across the floor. Lestrade grabbed it up and stared at it with mystified eyes.

'There's been a woman here,' he cried. 'It's a woman's wedding-ring.'

He held it out, as he spoke, upon the palm of his hand. We all gathered round him and gazed at it. There could be no doubt that that circlet of plain gold had once adorned the finger of a bride.

'This complicates matters,' said Gregson. 'Heaven knows, they were complicated enough before.'

'You're sure it doesn't simplify them?' observed Holmes. 'There's nothing to be learned by staring at it. What did you find in his pockets?'

'We have it all here,' said Gregson, pointing to a litter of objects upon one of the bottom steps of the stairs. 'A gold watch, No. 97163, by Barraud,[6] of London. Gold Albert chain,[7] very heavy and solid. Gold ring, with masonic device. Gold pin – bull-dog's head, with rubies as eyes. Russian leather card-case with cards of Enoch J. Drebber of Cleveland, corresponding with the E.J.D. upon the linen. No purse, but loose money to the extent of seven pounds thirteen. Pocket edition of Boccaccio's *Decameron*,[8] with name of Joseph Stangerson upon the fly-leaf. Two letters – one addressed to E. J. Drebber and one to Joseph Stangerson.'

'At what address?'

'American Exchange, Strand[9] – to be left till called for. They are both from the Guion Steamship Company,[10] and refer to the sailing of their boats from Liverpool. It is clear that this unfortunate man was about to return to New York.'

'Have you made any inquiries as to this man Stangerson?'

'I did it at once, sir,' said Gregson. 'I have had advertisements sent to all the newspapers, and one of my men has gone to the American Exchange, but he has not returned yet.'

'Have you sent to Cleveland?'

'We telegraphed this morning.'

'How did you word your inquiries?'

'We simply detailed the circumstances, and said that we should be glad of any information which could help us.'

'You did not ask for particulars on any point which appeared to you to be crucial?'

'I asked about Stangerson.'

'Nothing else? Is there no circumstance on which this whole case appears to hinge? Will you not telegraph again?'

'I have said all I have to say,' said Gregson, in an offended voice.

Sherlock Holmes chuckled to himself, and appeared to be about to make some remark, when Lestrade, who had been in the front room while we were holding this conversation in the hall, reappeared upon the scene, rubbing his hands in a pompous and self-satisfied manner.

'Mr Gregson,' he said, 'I have just made a discovery of the highest importance, and one which would have been overlooked had I not made a careful examination of the walls.'

The little man's eyes sparkled as he spoke, and he was evidently in a state of suppressed exultation at having scored a point against his colleague.

'Come here,' he said, bustling back into the room, the atmosphere of which felt clearer since the removal of its ghastly inmate. 'Now, stand there!'

He struck a match on his boot and held it up against the wall.

'Look at that!' he said, triumphantly.

I have remarked that the paper had fallen away in parts. In this particular corner of the room a large piece had peeled off, leaving a yellow square of coarse plastering. Across this bare space there was scrawled in blood-red letters a single word:

RACHE

'What do you think of that?' cried the detective, with the air of a showman exhibiting his show. 'This was overlooked because it was in the darkest corner of the room, and no one thought of looking there. The murderer has written it with his or her own blood. See this smear where it has trickled down the wall! That disposes of the idea of suicide anyhow. Why was that corner chosen to write it on? I will tell you. See that candle on the mantelpiece. It was lit at the time, and if it was lit this corner would be the brightest instead of the darkest portion of the wall.'

'And what does it mean now that you *have* found it?' asked Gregson in a deprecatory voice.

'Mean? Why, it means that the writer was going to put the female name Rachel, but was disturbed before he or she had time to finish. You mark my words, when this case comes to be cleared up you will find that a woman named Rachel has something to do with it. It's all very well for you to laugh, Mr Sherlock Holmes. You may be very smart and clever, but the old hound is the best, when all is said and done.'

'I really beg your pardon!' said my companion, who had ruffled the little man's temper by bursting into an explosion of laughter. 'You certainly have the credit of being the first of us to find this out and, as you say, it bears every mark of having been written by the other participant in last night's mystery. I have not had time to examine this room yet, but with your permission I shall do so now.'

As he spoke, he whipped a tape measure and a large round magnifying glass from his pocket. With these two implements he trotted noiselessly about the room, sometimes stopping, occasionally kneeling, and once lying flat upon his face. So engrossed was he with his occupation that he appeared to have forgotten our presence, for he chattered away to himself under his breath the whole time, keeping up a running fire of exclamations, groans, whistles, and little cries suggestive of encouragement and of hope. As I watched him I was irresistibly reminded of a pure-blooded, well-trained foxhound as it dashes backwards and forwards through the covert, whining in its eagerness, until it comes across the lost scent. For twenty minutes or more he continued his researches, measuring with the most exact care the distance between marks which were entirely invisible to me, and occasionally applying his tape to the walls in an equally incomprehensible manner. In one place he gathered up very carefully a little pile of grey dust from the floor, and packed it away in an envelope. Finally he examined with his glass the word upon the wall, going over every letter of it with the most minute exactness. This done, he appeared to be satisfied, for he replaced his tape and his glass in his pocket.

'They say that genius is an infinite capacity for taking pains,'[11] he remarked with a smile. 'It's a very bad definition, but it does apply to detective work.'

Gregson and Lestrade had watched the manoeuvres of their amateur companion with considerable curiosity and some contempt. They evidently failed to appreciate the fact, which I had begun to realize, that Sherlock Holmes's smallest actions were all directed towards some definite and practical end.

'What do you think of it, sir?' they both asked.

'It would be robbing you of the credit of the case if I was to presume to help you,' remarked my friend. 'You are doing so well now that it would be a pity for anyone to interfere.' There was a world of sarcasm in his voice as he spoke. 'If you will let me know how your investigations go,' he continued, 'I shall be happy to give you any help I can. In the meantime I should like to speak to the constable who found the body. Can you give me his name and address?'

Lestrade glanced at his notebook. 'John Rance,' he said. 'He is off duty now. You will find him at 46, Audley Court, Kennington Park Gate.'[12]

Holmes took a note of the address.

'Come along, Doctor,' he said; 'we shall go and look him up. I'll tell you one thing which may help you in the case,' he continued, turning to the two detectives. 'There has been murder done,[13] and the murderer was a man. He was more than six feet high, was in the prime of life,[14] had small feet for his height, wore coarse, square-toed boots and smoked a Trichinopoly cigar.[15] He came here with his victim in a four-wheeled cab, which was drawn by a horse with three old shoes and one new one on his off foreleg. In all probability the murderer had a florid face, and the finger-nails of his right hand were remarkably long. These are only a few indications, but they may assist you.'

Lestrade and Gregson glanced at each other with an incredulous smile.

'If this man was murdered, how was it done?' asked the former.

'Poison,' said Sherlock Holmes curtly, and strode off. 'One other thing, Lestrade,' he added, turning round at the door. ' "Rache" is the German for "revenge"; so don't lose your time by looking for Miss Rachel.'

With which Parthian shot[16] he walked away, leaving the two rivals open-mouthed behind him.

4

What John Rance Had to Tell

It was one o'clock when we left No. 3, Lauriston Gardens. Sherlock Holmes led me to the nearest telegraph office, whence he dispatched a long telegram. He then hailed a cab, and ordered the driver to take us to the address given us by Lestrade.

'There is nothing like first-hand evidence,' he remarked; 'as a matter of fact, my mind is entirely made up upon the case, but still we may as well learn all that is to be learned.'

'You amaze me, Holmes,' said I. 'Surely you are not as sure as you pretend to be of all those particulars which you gave.'

'There's no room for mistake,' he answered. 'The very first thing which I observed on arriving there was that a cab had made two ruts with its wheels close to the kerb. Now, up to last night, we have had no rain for a week, so that those wheels which left such a deep impression must have been there during the night. There were the marks of the horse's hoofs, too, the outline of one of which was far more clearly cut than that of the other three, showing that that was a new shoe. Since the cab was there after the rain began, and was not there at any time during the morning – I have Gregson's word for that – it follows that it must have been there during the night, and, therefore, that it brought those two individuals to the house.'

'That seems simple enough,' said I; 'but how about the other man's height?'

'Why, the height of a man, in nine cases out of ten, can be told from the length of his stride. It is a simple calculation enough, though there is no use my boring you with figures. I had this fellow's stride both on the clay outside and on the dust within. Then I had a way of checking my calculation. When a man writes on a wall, his instinct leads him to write about the level of his own eyes. Now that writing was just over six feet from the ground. It was child's play.'

'And his age?' I asked.

'Well, if a man can stride four and half feet without the smallest effort, he can't be quite in the sere and yellow.[1] That was the breadth of a puddle on the garden walk which he had evidently walked across. Patent-leather boots had gone round, and Square-toes had hopped over. There is no mystery about it at all. I am simply applying to ordinary life a few of those precepts of observation and deduction which I advocated in that article. Is there anything else that puzzles you?'

'The finger-nails and the Trichinopoly,' I suggested.

'The writing on the wall was done with a man's forefinger dipped in blood. My glass allowed me to observe that the plaster was slightly scratched in doing it, which would not have been the case if the man's nail had been trimmed. I gathered up some scattered ash from the floor. It was dark in colour and flakey – such an ash as is only made by a Trichinopoly. I have made a special study of cigar ashes – in fact, I have written a monograph upon the subject. I flatter myself that I can distinguish at a glance the ash of any known brand either of cigar or of tobacco. It is just in such details that the skilled detective differs from the Gregson and Lestrade type.'

'And the florid face?' I asked.

'Ah, that was a more daring shot, though I have no doubt that I was right. You must not ask me that at the present state of the affair.'

I passed my hand over my brow. 'My head is in a whirl,' I remarked; 'the more one thinks of it the more mysterious it grows. How came these two men – if there were two men – into an empty house? What has become of the cabman who drove them? How could one man compel another to take poison? Where did the blood come from? What was the object of the murderer, since robbery had no part in it? How came the woman's ring there? Above all, why should the second man write up the German word RACHE before decamping? I confess that I cannot see any possible way of reconciling all these facts.'

My companion smiled approvingly.

'You sum up the difficulties of the situation succinctly and well,' he said. 'There is much that is still obscure, though I have quite made up my mind on the main facts. As to poor Lestrade's discovery, it was simply a blind intended to put the police upon a wrong track, by suggesting Socialism and secret societies.[2] It was not done by a German. The A, if you noticed, was printed somewhat after the German fashion.[3] Now, a real German invariably prints in the Latin character,[4] so that we may safely say that this was not written by one, but by a clumsy imitator who overdid his part. It was simply a ruse to divert inquiry into a wrong channel. I'm not going to tell you much more of the case, Doctor. You know a conjurer gets no credit once he has explained his trick; and if I show you too much of my method of working, you will come to the conclusion that I am a very ordinary individual after all.'

'I shall never do that,' I answered; 'you have brought detection as near an exact science as it ever will be brought in this world.'

My companion flushed up with pleasure at my words, and the earnest way in which I uttered them. I had already observed that he was as sensitive to flattery on the score of his art as any girl could be of her beauty.

'I'll tell you one other thing,' he said. 'Patent-leathers and Square-toes came in the same cab, and they walked down the pathway together as friendly as possible – arm-in-arm, in all probability. When they got inside, they walked up and down the room – or rather, Patent-leathers stood still while Square-toes walked up and down. I could read all that in the dust; and I could read that as he walked he grew more and more excited. That is shown by the increased length of his strides. He was talking all the while, and working himself up, no doubt, into a fury. Then the tragedy occurred. I've told you all I know myself now, for the rest is mere surmise and conjecture. We have a good working basis, however, on which to start. We must hurry up, for I want to go to Hallé's concert[5] to hear Norman-Neruda[6] this afternoon.'

This conversation had occurred while our cab had been threading its way through a long succession of dingy streets and dreary byways. In the dingiest and dreariest of them our driver suddenly came to a stand. 'That's Audley Court in there,' he said, pointing to a narrow slit in the line of dead-coloured brick. 'You'll find me here when you come back.'

Audley Court was not an attractive locality. The narrow passage led us into a quadrangle paved with flags and lined by sordid dwellings. We picked our way among groups of dirty children, and through lines of discoloured linen, until we came to Number 46, the door of which was decorated with a small slip of brass on which the name Rance was engraved. On inquiry we found that the constable was in bed, and we were shown into a little front parlour to await his coming.

He appeared presently, looking a little irritable at being disturbed in his slumbers. 'I made my report at the office,' he said.

Holmes took a half-sovereign from his pocket[7] and played with it pensively. 'We thought that we should like to hear it all from your own lips,' he said.

'I shall be most happy to tell you anything I can,' the constable answered, with his eyes upon the little golden disc.

'Just let us hear it all in your own way as it occurred.'

Rance sat down on the horsehair sofa, and knitted his brows, as though determined not to omit anything in his narrative.

'I'll tell it ye from the beginning,' he said. 'My time is from ten at night to six in the morning. At eleven there was a fight at the White Hart;[8] but bar that all was quiet enough on the beat. At one o'clock it began to rain, and I met Harry Murcher – him who has the Holland Grove[9] beat – and we stood together at the corner of Henrietta Street[10] a-talkin'. Presently – maybe about two or a little after – I thought I would take a look round and see that all was right down the Brixton Road.[11] It was precious dirty and lonely. Not a soul did I meet all the way down, though a cab or two went past me. I was a-strollin' down, thinkin' between ourselves how uncommon handy a four of gin hot[12] would be, when suddenly the glint of a light caught my eye in the window of that same house. Now, I knew that them two houses in Lauriston Gardens was empty on account of him that owns them who won't have the drains seed to, though the very last tenant what lived in one of them died o' typhoid fever. I was knocked all in a heap, therefore, at seeing a light in the window, and I suspected as something was wrong. When I got to the door–'

'You stopped, and then walked back to the garden gate,' my companion interrupted. 'What did you do that for?'

Rance gave a violent jump, and stared at Sherlock Holmes with the utmost amazement upon his features.

'Why, that's true, sir,' he said; 'though how you come to know it, Heaven only knows. Ye see when I got up to the door, it was so still and lonesome, that I thought I'd be none the worse for someone with me. I ain't afeard of anything on this side o' the grave; but I thought that maybe it was him that died o' the typhoid inspecting the drains what killed him. The thought gave me a kind o' turn, and I walked back to the gate to see if I could see Murcher's lantern, but there wasn't no sign of him nor of anyone else.'

'There was no one in the street?'

'Not a livin' soul, sir, nor as much as a dog. Then I pulled myself together and went back and pushed the door open. All was quiet inside, so I went into the room where the light was a-burnin'. There was a candle flickerin' on the mantelpiece – a red wax one – and by its light I saw–'

'Yes, I know all that you saw. You walked round the room several times, and you knelt down by the body, and then you walked through and tried the kitchen door, and then–'

John Rance sprang to his feet with a frightened face and suspicion in his eyes. 'Where was you hid to see all that?' he cried. 'It seems to me that you knows a deal more than you should.'

Holmes laughed and threw his card across the table to the constable. 'Don't get arresting me for the murder,' he said. 'I am one of the hounds and not the wolf; Mr Gregson or Mr Lestrade will answer for that. Go on, though. What did you do next?'

Rance resumed his seat, without, however, losing his mystified expression. 'I went back to the gate and sounded my whistle. That brought Murcher and two more to the spot.'

'Was the street empty then?'

'Well, it was, as far as anybody that could be of any good goes.'

'What do you mean?'

The constable's features broadened into a grin. 'I've seen many a drunk chap in my time,' he said, 'but never anyone so cryin' drunk as that cove. He was at the gate when I came out, a-leanin' up ag'in the railings, and a-singin' at the pitch o' his lungs about Columbine's New-fangled Banner,[13] or some such stuff. He couldn't stand, far less help.'

'What sort of a man was he?' asked Sherlock Holmes.

John Rance appeared to be somewhat irritated at this digression. 'He was an uncommon drunk sort o' man,' he said. 'He'd ha' found hisself in the station if we hadn't been so took up.'

'His face – his dress – didn't you notice them?' Holmes broke in impatiently.

'I should think I did notice them, seeing that I had to prop him up – me and Murcher between us. He was a long chap, with a red face, the lower part muffled round–'

'That will do,' cried Holmes. 'What became of him?'

'We'd enough to do without lookin' after him,' the policeman said, in an aggrieved voice. 'I'll wager he found his way home all right.'

'How was he dressed?'

'A brown overcoat.'

'Had he a whip in his hand?'

'A whip – no.'

'He must have left it behind,' muttered my companion. 'You didn't happen to see or hear a cab after that?'

'No.'

'There's a half-sovereign for you,' my companion said, standing up and taking his hat. 'I am afraid, Rance, that you will never rise in the force. That head of yours should be for use as well as ornament. You might have gained your sergeant's stripes last night. The man whom you held in your hands is the man who holds the clue of this mystery, and whom we are seeking. There is no use of arguing about it now; I tell you that it is so. Come along, Doctor.'

We started off for the cab together, leaving our informant incredulous, but obviously uncomfortable.

'The blundering fool!' Holmes said, bitterly, as we drove back to our lodgings. 'Just to think of his having such an incomparable bit of luck, and not taking advantage of it.'

'I am rather in the dark still. It is true that the description of this man tallies with your idea of the second party in this mystery. But why should he come back to the house after leaving it? That is not the way of criminals.'

'The ring, man, the ring: that was what he came back for. If we have no other way of catching him, we can always bait our line with the ring. I shall have him, Doctor – I'll lay you two to one that I have him. I must thank you for it all. I might not have gone but for you, and so have missed the finest study I ever came across: a study in scarlet, eh? Why shouldn't we use a little art jargon? There's the scarlet thread[14] of murder running through the colourless skein of life, and our duty is to unravel it, and isolate it, and expose every inch of it. And now for lunch, and then for Norman-Neruda. Her attack and her bowing are splendid. What's that little thing of Chopin's she plays so magnificently:[15] Tra-la-la-lira-lira-lay.'

Leaning back in the cab, this amateur bloodhound carolled away like a lark while I meditated upon the many-sidedness of the human mind.

5

Our Advertisement Brings a Visitor

Our morning's exertions had been too much for my weak health, and I was tired out in the afternoon. After Holmes's departure for the concert, I lay down upon the sofa and endeavoured to get a couple of hours' sleep. It was a useless attempt. My mind had been too much excited by all that had occurred, and the strangest fancies and surmises crowded into it. Every time that I closed my eyes I saw before me the distorted, baboon-like countenance of the murdered man. So sinister was the impression which that face had produced upon me that I found it difficult to feel anything but gratitude for him who had removed its owner from the world. If ever human features bespoke vice of the most malignant type,[1] they were certainly those of Enoch J. Drebber, of Cleveland. Still, I recognized that justice must be done, and that the depravity of the victim was no condonement in the eyes of the law.

The more I thought of it the more extraordinary did my companion's hypothesis, that the man had been poisoned, appear. I remembered how he had sniffed his lips, and had no doubt that he had detected something which had given rise to the idea. Then, again, if not poison, what had caused the man's death, since there was neither wound nor marks of strangulation? But, on the other hand, whose blood was that which lay so thickly upon the floor? There were no signs of a struggle, nor had the victim any weapon with which he might have wounded an antagonist. As long as all these questions were unsolved, I felt that sleep would be no easy matter, either for Holmes or myself. His quiet, self-confident manner convinced me that he had already formed a theory which explained all the facts, though what it was I could not for an instant conjecture.

He was very late in returning – so late that I knew that the concert could not have detained him all the time. Dinner was on the table before he appeared.

'It was magnificent,' he said, as he took his seat. 'Do you remember what Darwin says about music?[2] He claims that the power of producing and appreciating it existed among the human race long before the power of speech was arrived at. Perhaps that is why we are so subtly influenced by it. There are vague memories in our souls of those misty centuries when the world was in its childhood.'

'That's rather a broad idea,' I remarked.

'One's ideas must be as broad as Nature if they are to interpret Nature,' he answered. 'What's the matter? You're not looking quite yourself. This Brixton Road affair has upset you.'

'To tell the truth, it has,' I said. 'I ought to be more case-hardened after my Afghan experiences. I saw my own comrades hacked to pieces at Maiwand without losing my nerve.'

'I can understand. There is a mystery about this which stimulates the imagination; where there is no imagination there is no horror. Have you seen the evening paper?'

'No.'

'It gives a fairly good account of the affair. It does not mention the fact that when the man was raised up a woman's wedding-ring fell upon the floor. It is just as well it does not.'

'Why?'

'Look at this advertisement,' he answered. 'I had one sent to every paper this morning immediately after the affair.'

He threw the paper across to me and I glanced at the place indicated. It was the first announcement in the 'Found' column. 'In Brixton Road, this morning,' it ran, 'a plain gold wedding-ring, found in the roadway between the White Hart Tavern and Holland Grove. Apply Dr Watson, 221B, Baker Street, between eight and nine this evening.'

'Excuse me using your name,' he said. 'If I used my own, some of these dunderheads would recognize it and want to meddle in the affair.'

'That is all right,' I answered. 'But supposing anyone applies, I have no ring.'

'Oh, yes, you have,' said he, handing me one. 'This will do very well. It is almost a facsimile.'

'And who do you expect will answer this advertisement?'

'Why, the man in the brown coat – our florid friend with the square toes. If he does not come himself, he will send an accomplice.'

'Would he not consider it as too dangerous?'

'Not at all. If my view of the case is correct, and I have every reason to believe that it is, this man would rather risk anything than lose the ring. According to my notion he dropped it while stooping over Drebber's body, and did not miss it at the time. After leaving the house he discovered his loss and hurried back, but found the police already in possession, owing to his own folly in leaving the candle burning. He had to pretend to be drunk in order to allay the suspicions which might have been aroused by his appearance at the gate. Now put yourself in that man's place. On thinking the matter over, it must have occurred to him that it was possible that he had lost the ring in the road after leaving the house. What would he do then? He would eagerly look out for the evening papers in the hope of seeing it among the articles found. His eye, of course, would alight upon this. He would be overjoyed. Why should he fear a trap? There would be no reason in his eyes why the finding of the ring should be connected with the murder. He would come. He will come. You shall see him within an hour.'

'And then?' I asked.

'Oh, you can leave me to deal with him then. Have you any arms?'

'I have my old service revolver[3] and a few cartridges.'

'You had better clean it and load it. He will be a desperate man; and though I shall take him unawares, it is as well to be ready for anything.'

I went to my bedroom and followed his advice. When I returned with the pistol, the table had been cleared, and Holmes was engaged in his favourite occupation of scraping upon his violin.

'The plot thickens,' he said, as I entered; 'I have just had an answer to my American telegram. My view of the case is the correct one.'

'And that is?' I asked eagerly.

'My fiddle would be the better for new strings,' he remarked. 'Put your pistol in your pocket. When the fellow comes, speak to him in an ordinary way. Leave the rest to me. Don't frighten him by looking at him too hard.'

'It is eight o'clock now,' I said, glancing at my watch.

'Yes. He will probably be here in a few minutes. Open the door slightly. That will do. Now put the key on the inside. Thank you! This is a queer old book I picked up at a stall yesterday – *De Jure inter Gentes*[4]– published in Latin at Liège in the Lowlands, in 1642. Charles's head was still firm on his shoulders[5] when this little brown-backed volume was struck off.'

'Who is the printer?'

'Philippe de Croy, whoever he may have been.[6] On the flyleaf, in very faded ink, is written "Ex libris Gulielmi Whyte." I wonder who William Whyte[7] was. Some pragmatical seventeenth-century lawyer, I suppose. His writing has a legal twist about it. Here comes our man, I think.'

As he spoke there was a sharp ring at the bell. Sherlock Holmes rose softly and moved his chair in the direction of the door. We heard the servant pass along the hall, and the sharp click of the latch as she opened it.

'Does Dr Watson live here?' asked a clear but rather harsh voice. We could not hear the servant's reply, but the door closed, and someone began to ascend the stairs. The footfall was an uncertain and shuffling one. A look of surprise passed over the face of my companion as he listened to it. It came slowly along the passage, and there was a feeble tap at the door.

'Come in,' I cried.

At my summons, instead of the man of violence whom we expected, a very old and wrinkled woman hobbled into the apartment. She appeared to be dazzled by the sudden blaze of light, and after dropping a curtsy, she stood blinking at us with her bleared eyes and fumbling in her pocket with nervous shaky fingers. I glanced at my companion, and his face had assumed such a disconsolate expression that it was all I could do to keep my countenance.

The old crone drew out an evening paper, and pointed at our advertisement. 'It's this as has brought me, good gentlemen,' she said, dropping another curtsy; 'a gold wedding-ring in the Brixton Road. It belongs to my girl Sally, as was married only this time twelve-month, which her husband is steward aboard a Union boat,[8] and what he'd say if he come 'ome and found her without her ring is more than I can think, he being short enough at the best o' times, but more especially when he has the drink. If it please you, she went to the circus last night along with –'

'Is that her ring?' I asked.

'The Lord be thanked!' cried the old woman; 'Sally will be a glad woman this night. That's the ring.'

'And what may your address be?' I inquired, taking up a pencil.

'13, Duncan Street, Houndsditch.[9] A weary way from here.'

'The Brixton Road does not lie between any circus and Houndsditch,' said Sherlock Holmes sharply.

The old woman faced round and looked keenly at him from her little red-rimmed eyes. 'The gentleman asked me for *my* address,' she said. 'Sally lives in lodgings at 3, Mayfield Place, Peckham.'[10]

'And your name is –?'

'My name is Sawyer – hers is Dennis, which Tom Dennis married her – and a smart, clean lad, too, as long as he's at sea, and no steward in the company more thought of; but when on shore, what with the women and what with liquor shops –'

'Here is your ring, Mrs Sawyer,' I interrupted, in obedience to a sign from my companion; 'it clearly belongs to your daughter, and I am glad to be able to restore it to the rightful owner.'

With many mumbled blessings and protestations of gratitude the old crone packed it away in her pocket, and shuffled off down the stairs. Sherlock Holmes sprang to his feet the moment that she was gone and rushed into his room. He returned in a few seconds enveloped in an ulster[11] and a cravat.[12] 'I'll follow her,' he said, hurriedly; 'she must be an accomplice, and will lead me to him. Wait up for me.' The hall door had hardly slammed behind our visitor before Holmes had descended the stair. Looking through the window I could see her walking feebly along the other side, while her pursuer dogged her some little distance behind. 'Either his whole theory is incorrect,' I thought to myself, 'or else he will be led now to the heart of the mystery.' There was no need for him to ask me to wait up for him, for I felt that sleep was impossible until I heard the result of his adventure.

It was close upon nine when he set out. I had no idea how long he might be, but I sat stolidly puffing at my pipe and skipping over the pages of Henri Murger's *Vie de Bohème*.[13] Ten o'clock passed, and I heard the footsteps of the maid as they pattered off to bed. Eleven, and the more stately tread of the landlady passed my door, bound for the same destination. It was close upon twelve before I heard the sharp sound of his latch-key. The instant he entered I saw by his face that he had not been successful. Amusement and chagrin seemed to be struggling for the mastery, until the former suddenly carried the day, and he burst into a hearty laugh.

'I wouldn't have the Scotland Yarders know it for the world,' he cried, dropping into his chair; 'I have chaffed them so much that they would never have let me hear the end of it. I can afford to laugh, because I know that I will be even with them in the long run.'

'What is it then?' I asked.

'Oh, I don't mind telling a story against myself. That creature had gone a little way when she began to limp and show every sign of being footsore. Presently she came to a halt, and hailed a four-wheeler which was passing. I managed to be close to her so as to hear the address, but I need not have been so anxious, for she sang it out loud enough to be heard at the other side of the street: "Drive to 13, Duncan Street, Houndsditch," she cried. This begins to look genuine. I thought, and having seen her safely inside, I perched myself behind. That's an art which every detective should be an expert at. Well, away we rattled, and never drew rein until we reached the street in question. I hopped off before we came to the door, and strolled down the street in an easy lounging way. I saw the cab pull up. The driver jumped down, and I saw him open the door and stand expectantly. Nothing came out though. When I reached him, he was groping about frantically in the empty cab, and giving vent to the finest assorted collection of oaths that ever I listened to. There was no sign or trace of his passenger, and I fear it will be some time before he gets his fare. On inquiring at Number 13 we found that the house belonged to a respectable paperhanger, named Keswick, and that no one of the name either of Sawyer or Dennis had ever been heard of there.'

'You don't mean to say,' I cried, in amazement, 'that that tottering, feeble old woman was able to get out of the cab while it was in motion, without either you or the driver seeing her?'

'Old woman be damned!' said Sherlock Holmes, sharply. 'We were the old women to be so taken in. It must have been a young man, and an active one, too, besides being an incomparable actor. The get-up was inimitable. He saw that he was followed, no doubt, and used this means of giving me the slip. It shows that the man we are after is not as lonely as I imagined he was, but has friends who are ready to risk something for him. Now, Doctor, you are looking done-up. Take my advice and turn in.'

I was certainly feeling very weary, so I obeyed his injunction. I left Holmes seated in front of the smouldering fire, and long into the watches of the night I heard the low, melancholy wailings of his violin, and knew that he was still pondering over the strange problem which he had set himself to unravel.

6

Tobias Gregson Shows What He Can Do

The papers next day were full of the 'Brixton Mystery', as they termed it. Each had a long account of the affair, and some had leaders upon it in addition. There was some information in them which was new to me. I still retain in my scrap-book numerous clippings and extracts bearing upon the case. Here is a condensation of a few of them:

The *Daily Telegraph* remarked that in the history of crime there had seldom been a tragedy which presented stranger features. The German name of the victim, the absence of all other motive, and the sinister inscription on the wall, all pointed to its perpetration by political refugees and revolutionists. The Socialists had many branches in America, and the deceased had, no doubt, infringed their unwritten laws, and been tracked down by them. After alluding airily to the Vehmgericht,[1] aqua tofana,[2] Carbonari,[3] the Marchioness de Brinvilliers,[4] the Darwinian theory,[5] the principles of Malthus,[6] and the Ratcliff Highway murders,[7] the article concluded by admonishing the Government and advocating a closer watch over foreigners in England.

The *Standard* commented upon the fact that lawless outrages of the sort usually occurred under a Liberal Administration.[8] They arose from the unsettling of the minds of the masses, and the consequent weakening of all authority. The deceased was an American gentleman who had been residing for some weeks in the Metropolis. He had stayed at the boarding-house of Madame Charpentier, in Torquay Terrace, Camberwell.[9] He was accompanied in his travels by his private secretary, Mr Joseph Stangerson. The two bade adieu to their landlady upon Tuesday, the 4th inst.,[10] and departed to Euston Station[11] with the avowed intention of catching the Liverpool express.

They were afterwards seen together upon the platform. Nothing more is known of them until Mr Drebber's body was, as recorded, discovered in an empty house in the Brixton Road, many miles from Euston. How he came there, or how he met his fate, are questions which are still involved in mystery. Nothing is known of the whereabouts of Stangerson. We are glad to learn that Mr Lestrade and Mr Gregson, of Scotland Yard, are both engaged upon the case, and it is confidently anticipated that these well-known officers will speedily throw light upon the matter.

The *Daily News* observed that there was no doubt as to the crime being a political one. The despotism and hatred of Liberalism which animated the Continental Governments had had the effect of driving to our shores a number of men who might have made excellent citizens were they not soured by the recollection of all that they had undergone. Among these men there was a stringent code of honour, any infringement of which was punished by death. Every effort should be made to find the secretary, Stangerson, and to ascertain some particulars of the habits of the deceased. A great step had been gained by the discovery of the address of the house at which he had boarded – a result which was entirely due to the acuteness and energy of Mr Gregson of Scotland Yard.

Sherlock Holmes and I read these notices over together at breakfast, and they appeared to afford him considerable amusement.

'I told you that, whatever happened, Lestrade and Gregson would be sure to score.'

'That depends on how it turns out.'

'Oh, bless you, it doesn't matter in the least. If the man is caught, it will be *on account* of their exertions; if he escapes, it will be *in spite* of their exertions. It's heads I win and tails you lose. Whatever they do, they will have followers. "Un sot trouve toujours un plus sot qui l'admire." '[12]

'What on earth is that?' I cried, for at this moment there came the pattering of many steps in the hall and on the stairs, accompanied by audible expressions of disgust upon the part of our landlady.

'It's the Baker Street division of the detective police force,' said my companion gravely; and as he spoke there rushed into the room half a dozen of the dirtiest and most ragged street Arabs that ever I clapped eyes on.

' 'Tention!' cried Holmes, in a sharp tone, and the six dirty scoundrels stood in a line like so many disreputable statuettes. 'In future you shall send up Wiggins alone to report, and the rest of you must wait in the street. Have you found it, Wiggins?'

'No, sir, we hain't,' said one of the youths.

'I hardly expected you would. You must keep on until you do. Here are your wages.' He handed each of them a shilling. 'Now, off you go, and come back with a better report next time.'

He waved his hand, and they scampered away downstairs like so many rats, and we heard their shrill voices next moment in the street.

'There's more work to be got out of one of those little beggars than out of a dozen of the force,' Holmes remarked. 'The mere sight of an official-looking person seals men's lips. These youngsters, however, go everywhere, and hear everything. They are as sharp as needles, too; all they want is organization.'

'Is it on this Brixton case that you are employing them?' I asked.

'Yes; there is a point which I wish to ascertain. It is merely a matter of time. Hullo! we are going to hear some news now with a vengeance! Here is Gregson coming down the road with beatitude written upon every feature of his face. Bound for us, I know. Yes, he is stopping. There he is!'

There was a violent peal at the bell, and in a few seconds the fair-haired detective came up the stairs, three steps at a time, and burst into our sitting-room.

'My dear fellow,' he cried, wringing Holmes's unresponsive hand, 'congratulate me! I have made the whole thing as clear as day.'

A shade of anxiety seemed to me to cross my companion's expressive face.

'Do you mean that you are on the right track?' he asked.

'The right track! Why, sir, we have the man under lock and key.'

'And his name is?'

'Arthur Charpentier, sub-lieutenant in Her Majesty's Navy,' cried Gregson pompously, rubbing his fat hands and inflating his chest.

Sherlock Holmes gave a sigh of relief and relaxed into a smile.

'Take a seat, and try one of these cigars,' he said. 'We are anxious to know how you managed it. Will you have some whisky and water?'

'I don't mind if I do,' the detective answered. 'The tremendous exertions which I have gone through during the last day or two have worn me out. Not so much bodily exertion, you understand, as the strain upon the mind. You will appreciate that, Mr Sherlock Holmes, for we are both brainworkers.'

'You do me too much honour,' said Holmes gravely. 'Let us hear how you arrived at this most gratifying result.'

The detective seated himself in the arm-chair, and puffed complacently at his cigar. Then suddenly he slapped his thigh in a paroxysm of amusement.

'The fun of it is,' he cried, 'that that fool Lestrade, who thinks himself so smart, has gone off upon the wrong track altogether. He is after the secretary Stangerson, who had no more to do with the crime than the babe unborn. I have no doubt that he has caught him by this time.'

The idea tickled Gregson so much that he laughed until he choked.

'And how did you get your clue?'

'Ah, I'll tell you all about it. Of course, Doctor Watson, this is strictly between ourselves. The first difficulty which we had to contend with was the finding of this American's antecedents. Some people would have waited until their advertisements were answered, or until parties came forward and volunteered information. That is not Tobias Gregson's way of going to work. You remember the hat beside the dead man?'

'Yes,' said Holmes; 'by John Underwood and Sons, 129, Camberwell Road.'

Gregson looked quite crestfallen.

'I had no idea that you noticed that,' he said. 'Have you been there?'

'No.'

'Ha!' cried Gregson, in a relieved voice; 'you should never neglect a chance, however small it may seem.'

'To a great mind, nothing is little,' remarked Holmes, sententiously.

'Well, I went to Underwood, and asked him if he had sold a hat of that size and description. He looked over his books, and came on it at once. He had sent the hat to a Mr Drebber, residing at Charpentier's Boarding Establishment, Torquay Terrace. Thus I got his address.'

'Smart – very smart!' murmured Sherlock Holmes.

'I next called upon Madame Charpentier,' continued the detective. 'I found her very pale and distressed. Her daughter was in the room, too – an uncommonly fine girl she is, too; she was looking red about the eyes and her lips trembled as I spoke to her. That didn't escape my notice. I began to smell a rat. You know that feeling, Mr Sherlock Holmes, when you come upon the right scent – a kind of thrill in your nerves. "Have you heard of the mysterious death of your late boarder Mr Enoch J. Drebber, of Cleveland?" I asked.

'The mother nodded. She didn't seem able to get out a word. The daughter burst into tears. I felt more than ever that these people knew something of the matter.

' "At what o'clock did Mr Drebber leave your house for the train?" I asked.

' "At eight o'clock," she said, gulping in her throat to keep down her agitation. "His secretary, Mr Stangerson, said that there were two trains – one at 9.15 and one at 11. He was to catch the first."

' "And was that the last which you saw of him?"

'A terrible change came over the woman's face as I asked the question. Her features turned perfectly livid. It was some seconds before she could get out the single word "Yes" – and when it did come it was in a husky, unnatural tone.

'There was a silence for a moment, and then the daughter spoke in a calm, clear voice.

' "No good can ever come of falsehood, mother," she said. "Let us be frank with this gentleman. We *did* see Mr Drebber again."

' "God forgive you!" cried Madame Charpentier, throwing up her hands, and sinking back in her chair. "You have murdered your brother."

' "Arthur would rather that we spoke the truth," the girl answered firmly.

' "You had best tell me all about it now," I said. "Half-confidences are worse than none. Besides, you do not know how much we know of it." .

' "On your head be it, Alice!" cried her mother; and then, turning to me: "I will tell you all, sir. Do not imagine that my agitation on behalf of my son arises from any fear lest he should have had a hand in this terrible affair. He is utterly innocent of it. My dread is, however, that in your eyes and in the eyes of others he may appear to be compromised. That, however, is surely impossible. His high character, his profession, his antecedents would all forbid it."

' "Your best way is to make a clean breast of the facts," I answered. "Depend upon it, if your son is innocent he will be none the worse."

' "Perhaps, Alice, you had better leave us together," she said, and her daughter withdrew. "Now, sir," she continued, "I had no intention of telling you all this, but since my poor daughter has disclosed it I have no alternative. Having once decided to speak, I will tell you all without omitting any particular."

' "It is your wisest course," said I.

' "Mr Drebber has been with us nearly three weeks. He and his secretary, Mr Stangerson, had been travelling on the Continent. I noticed a 'Copenhagen' label upon each of their trunks, showing that that had been their last stopping place. Stangerson was a quiet, reserved man, but his employer, I am sorry to say, was far otherwise. He was coarse in his habits and brutish in his ways. The very night of his arrival he became very much the worse for drink, and, indeed, after twelve o'clock in the day he could hardly ever be said to be sober. His manners towards the maid-servants were disgustingly free and familiar. Worst of all, he speedily assumed the same attitude towards my daughter Alice, and spoke to her more than once in a way which, fortunately, she is too innocent to understand. On one occasion he actually seized her in his arms and embraced her – an outrage which caused his own secretary to reproach him for his unmanly conduct."

' "But why did you stand all this?" I asked. "I suppose that you can get rid of your boarders when you wish."

'Madame Charpentier blushed at my pertinent question. "Would to God that I had given him notice on the very day that he came," she said. "But it was a sore temptation. They were paying a pound a day each – fourteen pounds a week, and this is the slack season. I am

55

a widow, and my boy in the Navy has cost me much. I grudged to lose the money. I acted for the best. This last was too much, however, and I gave him notice to leave on account of it. That was the reason of his going."

' "Well?"

' "My heart grew light when I saw him drive away. My son is on leave just now, but I did not tell him anything of all this, for his temper is violent, and he is passionately fond of his sister. When I closed the door behind them a load seemed to be lifted from my mind. Alas, in less than an hour there was a ring at the bell, and I learned that Mr Drebber had returned. He was much excited, and evidently the worse for drink. He forced his way into the room, where I was sitting with my daughter, and made some incoherent remark about having missed the train. He then turned to Alice, and before my very face proposed to her that she should fly with him. 'You are of age,' he said, 'and there is no law to stop you. I have money enough and to spare. Never mind the old girl here, but come along with me now straight away. You shall live like a princess.' Poor Alice was so frightened that she shrunk away from him, but he caught her by the wrist and endeavoured to draw her towards the door. I screamed, and at that moment my son Arthur came into the room. What happened then I do not know. I heard oaths and the confused sounds of a scuffle. I was too terrified to raise my head. When I did look up I saw Arthur standing in the doorway laughing, with a stick in his hand. 'I don't think that fine fellow will trouble us again,' he said. 'I will just go after him and see what he does with himself.' With those words he took his hat and started off down the street. The next morning we heard of Mr Drebber's mysterious death."

'This statement came from Madame Charpentier's lips with many gasps and pauses. At times she spoke so low that I could hardly catch the words. I made shorthand notes of all that she said, however, so that there should be no possibility of a mistake.'

'It's quite exciting,' said Sherlock Holmes, with a yawn. 'What happened next?'

'When Madame Charpentier paused,' the detective continued, 'I saw that the whole case hung upon one point. Fixing her with my eye in a way which I always found effective with women, I asked her at what hour her son returned.

' "I do not know," she answered.

' "Not know?"

' "No; he has a latch-key, and he let himself in."

' "After you went to bed?"

' "Yes."

' "When did you go to bed?"

' "About eleven."

' "So your son was gone at least two hours?"

' "Yes."

' "Possibly four or five?"

' "Yes."

' "What was he doing during that time?"

' "I do not know," she answered, turning white to her very lips.

'Of course after that there was nothing more to be done. I found out where Lieutenant Charpentier was, took two officers with me, and arrested him. When I touched him on the shoulder and warned him to come quietly with us, he answered us as bold as brass: "I suppose you are arresting me for being concerned in the death of that scoundrel Drebber," he said. We had said nothing to him about it, so that his alluding to it had a most suspicious aspect.'

'Very,' said Holmes.

'He still carried the heavy stick which the mother described him as having with him when he followed Drebber. It was a stout oak cudgel.'

'What is your theory, then?'

'Well, my theory is that he followed Drebber as far as the Brixton Road. When there, a fresh altercation arose between them, in the course of which Drebber received a blow from the stick, in the pit of the stomach perhaps, which killed him without leaving any mark. The night was so wet that no one was about, so Charpentier dragged the body of his victim into the empty house. As to the candle, and the blood, and the writing on the wall, and the ring, they may all be so many tricks to throw the police on to the wrong scent.'

'Well done!' said Holmes in an encouraging voice. 'Really, Gregson, you are getting along. We shall make something of you yet.'

'I flatter myself that I have managed it rather neatly,' the detective answered proudly. 'The young man volunteered a statement, in which he said that after following Drebber some time, the latter perceived him, and took a cab in order to get away from him. On his way home he met an old shipmate, and took a long walk with him. On being asked where this old shipmate lived, he was unable to give any satisfactory reply. I think the whole case fits together uncommonly well. What amuses me is to think of Lestrade, who had started off upon the wrong scent. I am afraid he won't make much of it. Why, by Jove, here's the very man himself!'

It was indeed Lestrade, who had ascended the stairs while we were talking, and who now entered the room. The assurance and jauntiness which generally marked his demeanour and dress were, however, wanting. His face was disturbed and troubled, while his clothes were disarranged and untidy. He had evidently come with the intention of consulting with Sherlock Holmes, for on perceiving his colleague he appeared to be embarrassed and put out. He stood in the centre of the room, fumbling nervously with his hat and uncertain what to do. 'This is a most extraordinary case,' he said at last – 'a most incomprehensible affair.'

'Ah, you find it so, Mr Lestrade!' cried Gregson, triumphantly. 'I thought you would come to that conclusion. Have you managed to find the secretary, Mr Joseph Stangerson?'

'The secretary, Mr Joseph Stangerson,' said Lestrade gravely, 'was murdered at Halliday's Private Hotel about six o'clock this morning.'

7

Light in the Darkness

The intelligence with which Lestrade greeted us was so momentous
and so unexpected that we were all three fairly dumbfounded. Gregson
sprang out of his chair and upset the remainder of his whisky and water.
I stared in silence at Sherlock Holmes, whose lips were compressed and
his brows drawn down over his eyes.

'Stangerson too!' he muttered. 'The plot thickens.'

'It was quite thick enough before,' grumbled Lestrade, taking a
chair. 'I seem to have dropped into a sort of council of war.'

'Are you – are you sure of this piece of intelligence?' stammered
Gregson.

'I have just come from his room,' said Lestrade. 'I was the first to
discover what had occurred.'

'We have been hearing Gregson's view of the matter,' Holmes
observed. 'Would you mind letting us know what you have seen and
done?'

'I have no objection,' Lestrade answered, seating himself. 'I freely
confess that I was of the opinion that Stangerson was concerned in
the death of Drebber. This fresh development has shown me that I
was completely mistaken. Full of the one idea, I set myself to find out
what had become of the secretary. They had been seen together at
Euston Station about half past eight on the evening of the third. At
two in the morning Drebber had been found in the Brixton Road.
The question which confronted me was to find out how Stangerson
had been employed between 8.30 and the time of the crime, and what
had become of him afterwards. I telegraphed to Liverpool, giving a
description of the man, and warning them to keep a watch upon the

American boats. I then set to work calling upon all the hotels and lodging-houses in the vicinity of Euston. You see, I argued that if Drebber and his companion had become separated, the natural course for the latter would be to put up somewhere in the vicinity for the night, and then to hang about the station again next morning.'

'They would be likely to agree on some meeting place beforehand,' remarked Holmes.

'So it proved. I spent the whole of yesterday evening in making inquiries entirely without avail. This morning I began very early, and at eight o'clock I reached Halliday's Private Hotel, in Little George Street. On my inquiry as to whether a Mr Stangerson was living there, they at once answered me in the affirmative.

' "No doubt you are the gentleman whom he was expecting," they said. "He has been waiting for a gentleman for two days."

' "Where is he now?" I asked.

' "He is upstairs in bed. He wished to be called at nine."

' "I will go up and see him at once," I said.

'It seemed to me that my sudden appearance might shake his nerves and lead him to say something unguarded. The Boots volunteered to show me the room: it was on the second floor, and there was a small corridor leading up to it. The Boots pointed out the door to me, and was about to go downstairs again when I saw something that made me feel sickish, in spite of my twenty years' experience. From under the door there curled a little red ribbon of blood, which had meandered across the passage and formed a little pool along the skirting at the other side. I gave a cry, which brought the Boots back. He nearly fainted when he saw it. The door was locked on the inside, but we put our shoulders to it, and knocked it in. The window of the room was open, and beside the window all huddled up, lay the body of a man in his nightdress. He was quite dead, and had been for some time, for his limbs were rigid and cold. When we turned him over, the Boots recognized him at once as being the same gentleman who had engaged the room under the name of Joseph Stangerson. The cause of death was a deep stab in the left side, which must have penetrated the heart. And now comes the strangest part of the affair. What do you suppose was above the murdered man?'

I felt a creeping of the flesh, and a presentiment of coming horror, even before Sherlock Holmes answered.

'The word RACHE, written in letters of blood,' he said.

'That was it,' said Lestrade, in an awe-struck voice; and we were all silent for a while.

There was something so methodical and so incomprehensible about the deeds of this unknown assassin, that it imparted a fresh ghastliness to his crimes. My nerves, which were steady enough on the field of battle, tingled as I thought of it.

'The man was seen,' continued Lestrade. 'A milk boy, passing on his way to the dairy, happened to walk down the lane which leads from the mews at the back of the hotel. He noticed that a ladder, which usually lay there, was raised against one of the windows of the second floor, which was wide open. After passing, he looked back and saw a man descend the ladder. He came down so quietly and openly that the boy imagined him to be some carpenter or joiner at work in the hotel. He took no particular notice of him, beyond thinking in his own mind that it was early for him to be at work. He has an impression that the man was tall, had a reddish face, and was dressed in a long, brownish coat. He must have stayed in the room some little time after the murder, for we found blood-stained water in the basin, where he had washed his hands, and marks on the sheets where he had deliberately wiped his knife.'

I glanced at Holmes on hearing the description of the murderer which tallied so exactly with his own. There was, however, no trace of exultation or satisfaction upon his face.

'Did you find nothing in the room which could furnish a clue to the murderer?' he asked.

'Nothing. Stangerson had Drebber's purse in his pocket, but it seems that this was usual, as he did all the paying. There was eighty-odd pounds in it, but nothing had been taken. Whatever the motives of these extraordinary crimes, robbery is certainly not one of them. There were no papers or memoranda in the murdered man's pocket, except a single telegram, dated from Cleveland about a month ago, and containing the words, "J. H. is in Europe." There was no name appended to this message.'

'And there was nothing else?' Holmes asked.

'Nothing of any importance. The man's novel, with which he had read himself to sleep, was lying upon the bed, and his pipe was on a chair beside him. There was a glass of water on the table, and on the window-sill a small chip ointment box containing a couple of pills.'

Sherlock Holmes sprang from his chair with an exclamation of delight.

'The last link,' he cried, exultantly. 'My case is complete.'

The two detectives stared at him in amazement.

'I have now in my hands,' my companion said, confidently, 'all the threads which have formed such a tangle. There are, of course, details to be filled in, but I am as certain of all the main facts, from the time that Drebber parted from Stangerson at the station, up to the discovery of the body of the latter, as if I had seen them with my own eyes. I will give you a proof of my knowledge. Could you lay your hand upon those pills?'

'I have them,' said Lestrade, producing a small white box; 'I took them and the purse and the telegram, intending to have them put in a place of safety at the Police Station. It was the merest chance my taking these pills, for I am bound to say I do not attach any importance to them.'

'Give them here,' said Holmes. 'Now, Doctor,' turning to me, 'are those ordinary pills?'

They certainly were not. They were of a pearly grey colour, small, round, and almost transparent against the light. 'From their lightness and transparency, I should imagine that they are soluble in water,' I remarked.

'Precisely so,' answered Holmes. 'Now would you mind going down and fetching that poor little devil of a terrier which has been bad so long, and which the landlady wanted you to put out of its pain yesterday.'

I went downstairs and carried the dog upstairs in my arms. Its laboured breathing and glazing eye showed that it was not far from its end. Indeed, its snow-white muzzle proclaimed that it had already exceeded the usual term of canine existence. I placed it upon a cushion on the rug.

'I will now cut one of these pills in two,' said Holmes, and drawing his penknife he suited the action to the word. 'One half we return into the box for future purposes. The other half I will place in this wine-glass, in which is a teaspoonful of water. You perceive that our friend the Doctor is right, and that it readily dissolves.'

'This may be very interesting,' said Lestrade, in the injured tone of one who suspects that he is being laughed at; 'I cannot see, however, what it has to do with the death of Mr Joseph Stangerson.'

'Patience, my friend, patience! You will find in time that it has everything to do with it. I shall now add a little milk to make the mixture palatable, and on presenting it to the dog we find that he laps it up readily enough.'

As he spoke he turned the contents of the wine-glass into a saucer and placed it in front of the terrier, who speedily licked it dry. Sherlock Holmes's earnest demeanour had so far convinced us that we all sat in silence, watching the animal intently, and expecting some start-ling effect. None such appeared, however. The dog continued to lie stretched upon the cushion, breathing in a laboured way but apparently neither the better nor the worse for its draught.

Holmes had taken out his watch, and as minute followed minute without result, an expression of the utmost chagrin and disappoint-ment appeared upon his features. He gnawed his lip, drummed his fingers upon the table, and showed every other symptom of acute impatience. So great was his emotion that I felt sincerely sorry for him, while the two detectives smiled derisively, by no means displeased at this check which he had met.

'It can't be a coincidence,' he cried, at last springing from his chair and pacing wildly up and down the room; 'it is impossible that it should be a mere coincidence. The very pills which I suspected in the case of Drebber are actually found after the death of Stangerson. And yet they are inert. What can it mean? Surely my whole chain of reasoning cannot have been false. It is impossible! And yet this wretched dog is none the worse. Ah, I have it! I have it!' With a perfect shriek of delight he rushed to the box, cut the other pill in two, dissolved it, added milk, and presented it to the terrier. The unfortu-nate creature's tongue seemed hardly to have been moistened in it before it gave a convulsive shiver in every limb, and lay as rigid and lifeless as if it had been struck by lightning.

Sherlock Holmes drew a long breath, and wiped the perspiration from his forehead. 'I should have more faith,' he said; 'I ought to know by this time that when a fact appears to be opposed to a long train of deductions, it invariably proves to be capable of bearing some other interpretation. Of the two pills in the box, one was of the most deadly poison, and the other was entirely harmless. I ought to have known that before ever I saw the box at all.'

This last statement appeared to me to be so startling that I could hardly believe that he was in his sober senses. There was the dead dog, however, to prove that his conjecture had been correct. It seemed to me that the mists in my own mind were gradually clearing away, and I began to have a dim, vague perception of the truth.

'All this seems strange to you,' continued Holmes, 'because you failed at the beginning of the inquiry to grasp the importance of the single real clue which was presented to you. I had the good fortune to seize upon that, and everything which has occurred since then has served to confirm my original supposition, and, indeed, was the logical sequence of it. Hence things which have perplexed you and made the case more obscure have served to enlighten me and to strengthen my conclusions. It is a mistake to confound strangeness with mystery. The most commonplace crime is often the most mysterious, because it presents no new or special features from which deductions may be drawn. This murder would have been infinitely more difficult to unravel had the body of the victim been simply found lying in the roadway without any of those *outré* and sensational accompaniments which have rendered it remarkable. These strange details, far from making the case more difficult, have really had the effect of making it less so.'

Mr Gregson, who had listened to this address with considerable impatience, could contain himself no longer. 'Look here, Mr Sherlock Holmes,' he said, 'we are all ready to acknowledge that you are a smart man, and that you have your own methods of working. We want something more than mere theory and preaching now, though. It is a case of taking the man. I have made my case out, and it seems

I was wrong. Young Charpentier could not have been engaged in this second affair. Lestrade went after his man, Stangerson, and it appears that he was wrong too. You have thrown out hints here, and hints there, and seem to know more than we do, but the time has come when we feel that we have a right to ask you straight how much you do know of the business. Can you name the man who did it?'

'I cannot help feeling that Gregson is right, sir,' remarked Lestrade. 'We have both tried, and we have both failed. You have remarked more than once since I have been in the room that you had all the evidence which you require. Surely you will not withhold it any longer.'

'Any delay in arresting the assassin,' I observed, 'might give him time to perpetrate some fresh atrocity.'

Thus pressed by us all, Holmes showed signs of irresolution. He continued to walk up and down the room with his head sunk on his chest and his brows drawn down, as was his habit when lost in thought.

'There will be no more murders,' he said at last, stopping abruptly and facing us. 'You can put that consideration out of the question. You have asked me if I know the name of the assassin. I do. The mere knowing of his name is a small thing, however, compared with the power of laying our hands upon him. This I expect very shortly to do. I have good hopes of managing it through my own arrangements; but it is a thing which needs delicate handling, for we have a shrewd and desperate man to deal with, who is supported, as I have had occasion to prove, by another who is as clever as himself. As long as this man has no idea that anyone can have a clue there is some chance of securing him; but if he had the slightest suspicion, he would change his name, and vanish in an instant among the four million inhabitants of this great city. Without meaning to hurt either of your feelings, I am bound to say that I consider these men to be more than a match for the official force, and that is why I have not asked your assistance. If I fail, I shall, of course, incur all the blame due to this omission; but that I am prepared for. At present I am ready to promise that the instant that I can communicate with you without endangering my own combinations, I shall do so.'

Gregson and Lestrade seemed to be far from satisfied by this assurance, or by the depreciating allusion to the detective police. The former had flushed up to the roots of his flaxen hair, while the other's beady eyes glistened with curiosity and resentment. Neither of them had time to speak, however, before there was a tap at the door, and the spokesman of the street Arabs, young Wiggins, introduced his insignificant and unsavoury person.

'Please, sir,' he said, touching his forelock, 'I have the cab downstairs.'

'Good boy,' said Holmes, blandly. 'Why don't you introduce this pattern at Scotland Yard?' he continued, taking a pair of steel handcuffs from a drawer. 'See how beautifully the spring works. They fasten in an instant.'

'The old pattern is good enough,' remarked Lestrade, 'if we can only find the man to put them on.'

'Very good, very good,' said Holmes, smiling. 'The cabman may as well help me with my boxes. Just ask him to step up, Wiggins.'

I was surprised to find my companion speaking as though he were about to set out on a journey, since he had not said anything to me about it. There was a small portmanteau in the room, and this he pulled out and began to strap. He was busily engaged at it when the cabman entered the room.

'Just give me a help with this buckle, cabman,' he said, kneeling over his task, and never turning his head.

The fellow came forward with a somewhat sullen, defiant air and put down his hands to assist. At that instant there was a sharp click, the jangling of metal, and Sherlock Holmes sprang to his feet again.

'Gentlemen,' he cried, with flashing eyes, 'let me introduce you to Mr Jefferson Hope, the murderer of Enoch Drebber and of Joseph Stangerson.'

The whole thing occurred in a moment – so quickly that I had no time to realize it. I have a vivid recollection of that instant, of Holmes's triumphant expression and the ring of his voice, of the cabman's dazed, savage face, as he glared at the glittering handcuffs, which had appeared as if by magic upon his wrists. For a second or two we might have been a group of statues. Then with an inarticulate roar of fury, the prisoner wrenched himself free from Holmes's grasp, and hurled himself through the window. Woodwork and glass gave way before him; but before he got quite through, Gregson, Lestrade, and Holmes sprang upon him like so many staghounds. He was dragged back into the room, and then commenced a terrific conflict. So powerful and so fierce was he that the four of us were shaken off again and again. He appeared to have the convulsive strength of a man in an epileptic fit. His face and hands were terribly mangled by his passage through the glass, but loss of blood had no effect in diminishing his resistance. It was not until Lestrade succeeded in getting his hand inside his neck-cloth and half-strangling him that we made him realize that his struggles were of no avail; and even then we felt no security until we had pinioned his feet as well as his hands. That done, we rose to our feet breathless and panting.

'We have his cab,' said Sherlock Holmes. 'It will serve to take him to Scotland Yard. And now, gentlemen,' he continued, with a pleasant smile, 'we have reached the end of our little mystery. You are very welcome to put any questions that you like to me now, and there is no danger that I will refuse to answer them.'

PART TWO

The Country of the Saints

I

On the Great Alkali Plain

In the central portion of the great North American Continent there lies an arid and repulsive desert, which for many a long year served as a barrier against the advance of civilization. From the Sierra Nevada to Nebraska, and from the Yellowstone River in the north to the Colorado upon the south, is a region of desolation and silence. Nor is Nature always in one mood throughout this grim district. It comprises snowcapped and lofty mountains, and dark and gloomy valleys. There are swift-flowing rivers which dash through jagged canyons; and there are enormous plains, which in winter are white with snow, and in summer are grey with the saline alkali dust. They all preserve, however, the common characteristics of barrenness, inhospitality, and misery.

There are no inhabitants of this land of despair. A band of Pawnees[1] or of Blackfeet[2] may occasionally traverse it in order to reach other hunting-grounds, but the hardiest of the braves are glad to lose sight of those awesome plains, and to find themselves once more upon their prairies. The coyote skulks among the scrub, the buzzard flaps heavily through the air, and the clumsy grizzly bear lumbers through the dark ravines, and picks up such sustenance as it can amongst the rocks. These are the sole dwellers in the wilderness.

In the whole world there can be no more dreary view than that from the northern slope of the Sierra Blanco.[3] As far as the eye can reach stretches the great flat plain-land, all dusted over with patches of alkali, and intersected by clumps of the dwarfish chapparal bushes. On the extreme verge of the horizon lies a long chain of mountain peaks, with their rugged summits flecked with snow. In this great stretch of country there is no sign of life, nor of anything appertaining to life. There is no bird in the steel-blue heaven, no movement upon the dull, grey earth – above all, there is absolute silence. Listen as one may, there is no shadow of a sound in all that mighty wilderness: nothing but silence – complete and heart-subduing silence.

It has been said there is nothing appertaining to life upon the broad plain. That is hardly true. Looking down from the Sierra Blanco, one sees a pathway traced out across the desert, which winds away and is lost in the extreme distance. It is rutted with wheels and trodden down by the feet of many adventurers. Here and there are scattered white objects which glisten in the sun, and stand out against the dull deposit of alkali. Approach, and examine them! They are bones: some large and coarse, others smaller and more delicate. The former have belonged to oxen, and the latter to men. For fifteen hundred miles one may trace this ghastly caravan route by these scattered remains of those who had fallen by the wayside.

Looking down on this very scene, there stood upon the fourth of May, eighteen hundred and forty-seven,[4] a solitary traveller. His appearance was such that he might have been the very genius or demon of the region. An observer would have found it difficult to say whether he was nearer to forty or to sixty. His face was lean and haggard, and the brown parchment-like skin was drawn tightly over the projecting bones; his long, brown hair and beard were all flecked and dashed with white; his eyes were sunken in his head, and burned with an unnatural lustre; while the hand which grasped his rifle was hardly more fleshy than that of a skeleton. As he stood, he leaned upon his weapon for support, and yet his tall figure and the massive framework of his bones suggested a wiry and vigorous constitution. His gaunt face, however, and his clothes, which hung so baggily over his shrivelled limbs, proclaimed what it was that gave him that senile and decrepit appearance. The man was dying – dying from hunger and from thirst.

He had toiled painfully down the ravine, and on to this little elevation, in the vain hope of seeing some signs of water. Now the great salt plain stretched before his eyes, and the distant belt of savage mountains, without a sign anywhere of plant or tree, which might indicate the presence of moisture. In all that broad landscape there was no gleam of hope. North, and east, and west he looked with wild, questioning eyes, and then he realized that his wanderings had come to an end, and that there, on that barren crag, he was about to die. 'Why not here, as well as in a feather bed, twenty years hence,' he muttered, as he seated himself in the shelter of a boulder.

Before sitting down, he had deposited upon the ground his useless rifle, and also a large bundle tied up in a grey shawl, which he had carried slung over his right shoulder. It appeared to be somewhat too heavy for his strength, for in lowering it, it came down on the ground with some little violence. Instantly there broke from the grey parcel a little moaning cry, and from it there protruded a small, scared face, with very bright brown eyes, and two little speckled dimpled fists.

'You've hurt me!' said a childish voice, reproachfully.

'Have I though,' the man answered penitently; 'I didn't go for to do it.' As he spoke he unwrapped the grey shawl and extricated a pretty little girl of about five years of age, whose dainty shoes and smart pink frock with its little linen apron all bespoke a mother's care. The child was pale and wan, but her healthy arms and legs showed that she had suffered less than her companion.

'How is it now?' he answered anxiously, for she was still rubbing the towsy golden curls which covered the back of her head.

'Kiss it and make it well,' she said, with perfect gravity, showing the injured part to him. 'That's what mother used to do. Where's mother?'

'Mother's gone. I guess you'll see her before long.'

'Gone, eh!' said the little girl. 'Funny, she didn't say goodbye; she 'most always did if she was just goin' over to auntie's for tea, and now she's been away three days. Say, it's awful dry, ain't it? Ain't there no water nor nothing to eat?'

'No, there ain't nothing, dearie. You'll just need to be patient awhile, and then you'll be all right. Put your head up agin' me like that, and then you'll feel bullier. It ain't easy to talk when your lips is like leather, but I guess I'd best let you know how the cards lie. What's that you've got?'

'Pretty things! fine things!' cried the little girl enthusiastically, holding up two glittering fragments of mica. 'When we goes back to home I'll give them to brother Bob.'

'You'll see prettier things than them soon,' said the man confidently. 'You just wait a bit. I was going to tell you though – you remember when we left the river?'

'Oh, yes.'

'Well, we reckoned we'd strike another river soon, d'ye see. But there was somethin' wrong; compasses, or map, or somethin', and it didn't turn up. Water ran out. Just except a little drop for the likes of you and – and –'

'And you couldn't wash yourself,' interrupted his companion gravely, staring up at his grimy visage.

'No, nor drink. And Mr Bender,[5] he was the fust to go, and then Indian Pete, and then Mrs McGregor, and then Johnny Hones, and then dearie, your mother.'

'Then mother's a deader too,' cried the little girl, dropping her face in her pinafore and sobbing bitterly.

'Yes, they all went except you and me. Then I thought there was some chance of water in this direction, so I heaved you over my shoulder and we tramped it together. It don't seem as though we've improved matters. There's an almighty small chance for us now!'

'Do you mean that we are going to die too?' asked the child. checking her sobs, and raising her tear-stained face.

'I guess that's about the size of it.'

'Why didn't you say so before?' she said, laughing gleefully. 'You gave me such a fright. Why, of course, now as long as we die we'll be with mother again.'

'Yes, you will, dearie.'

'And you too. I'll tell her how awful good you've been. I'll bet she meets us at the door of heaven with a big pitcher of water, and a lot of buckwheat cakes, hot, and toasted on both sides, like Bob and me was fond of. How long will it be first?'

'I don't know – not very long.' The man's eyes were fixed upon the northern horizon. In the blue vault of the heaven there had appeared three little specks which increased in size every moment, so rapidly did they approach. They speedily resolved themselves into three large birds, which circled over the heads of the two wanderers, and then settled upon some rocks which overlooked them. They were buzzards, the vultures of the west, whose coming is the forerunner of death.

'Cocks and hens,' cried the little girl gleefully, pointing at their ill-omened forms, and clapping her hands to make them rise. 'Say, did God make this country?'

'Of course He did,' said her companion, rather startled by this unexpected question.

'He made the country down in Illinois, and He made the Missouri,'[6] the little girl continued. 'I guess somebody else made the country in these parts. It's not nearly so well done. They forgot the water and the trees.'

'What would ye think of offering up prayer?' the man asked diffidently.

'It ain't night yet,' she answered.

'It don't matter. It ain't quite regular, but He won't mind that, you bet. You say over them ones that you used to say every night in the wagon when we was on the Plains.'

'Why don't you say some yourself?' the child asked, with wondering eyes.

'I disremember them,' he answered. 'I hain't said none since I was half the height o' that gun. I guess it's never too late. You say them out, and I'll stand by and come in on the choruses.'

'Then you'll need to kneel down, and me too,' she said, laying the shawl out for that purpose. 'You've got to put your hands up like this. It makes you feel kind of good.'

It was a strange sight, had there been anything but the buzzards to see it. Side by side on the narrow shawl knelt the two wanderers, the little prattling child and the reckless, hardened adventurer. Her chubby face and his haggard, angular visage were both turned up to the cloudless heaven in heartfelt entreaty to that dread Being with whom they were face to face, while the two voices – the one thin and clear, the other deep and harsh – united in the entreaty for mercy and forgiveness. The prayer finished, they resumed their seat in the shadow of the boulder until the child fell asleep, nestling upon the broad breast of her protector. He watched over her slumber for some time, but Nature proved to be too strong for him. For three days and three nights he had allowed himself neither rest nor repose. Slowly the eyelids drooped over the tired eyes, and the head sunk lower and lower upon the breast, until the man's grizzled beard was mixed with the gold tresses of his companion, and both slept the same deep and dreamless slumber.

Had the wanderer remained awake for another half-hour a strange sight would have met his eyes. Far away on the extreme verge of the alkali plain there rose up a little spray of dust, very slight at first, and hardly to be distinguished from the mists of the distance, but gradually growing higher and broader until it formed a solid, well-defined cloud. This cloud continued to increase in size until it became evident that it could only be raised by a great multitude of moving creatures. In more fertile spots the observer would have come to the conclusion that one of those great herds of bisons which graze upon the prairie land was approaching him. This was obviously impossible in these arid wilds. As the whirl of dust drew nearer to the solitary bluff upon which the two castaways were reposing, the canvas-covered tilts of wagons and the figures of armed horsemen began to show up through the haze, and the apparition revealed itself as being a great caravan upon its journey for the West. But what a caravan! When the head of it had reached the base of the mountains, the rear was not yet visible on the horizon. Right across the enormous plain stretched the straggling array, wagons and carts, men on horseback, and men on foot. Innumerable women who staggered along under burdens, and children who toddled beside the wagons or peeped out from under the white coverings. This was evidently no ordinary party of immigrants, but rather some nomad people who had been compelled from stress of circumstances to seek themselves a new country. There rose through the clear air a confused clattering and rumbling from this great mass of humanity, with the creaking of wheels and the neighing horses. Loud as it was, it was not sufficient to rouse the two tired wayfarers above them.

At the head of the column there rode a score or more of grave, iron-faced men, clad in sombre homespun garments and armed with rifles. On reaching the base of the bluff they halted, and held a short council among themselves.

'The wells are to the right, my brothers,' said one, a hard-lipped, clean-shaven man with grizzly hair.

'To the right of the Sierra Blanco – so we shall reach the Rio Grande,' said another.

'Fear not for water,' cried a third. 'He who could draw it from the rocks will not now abandon His chosen people.'

'Amen! amen!' responded the whole party.

They were about to resume their journey when one of the youngest and keenest-eyed uttered an exclamation and pointed up at the rugged crag above them. From its summit there fluttered a little wisp of pink, showing up hard and bright against the grey rocks behind. At the sight there was a general reining up of horses and unslinging of guns, while fresh horsemen came galloping up to reinforce the vanguard. The word 'Redskins' was on every lip.

'There can't be any number of Injuns here,' said the elderly man who appeared to be in command. 'We have passed the Pawnees, and there are no other tribes until we cross the great mountains.'

'Shall I go forward and see, Brother Stangerson,' asked one of the band.

'And I,' 'And I,' cried a dozen voices.

'Leave your horses below and we will await you here,' the Elder answered. In a moment the young fellows had dismounted, fastened their horses, and were ascending the precipitous slope which led up to the object which had excited their curiosity. They advanced rapidly and noiselessly, with the confidence and dexterity of practised scouts. The watchers from the plain below could see them flit from rock to rock until their figures stood out against the skyline. The young man who had first given alarm was leading them. Suddenly his followers saw him throw up his hands, as though overcome with astonishment, and on joining him they were affected in the same way by the sight which met their eyes.

On the little plateau which crowned the barren hill there stood a single giant boulder, and against this boulder there lay a tall man, long-bearded and hard-featured, but of an excessive thinness. His placid face and regular breathing showed that he was fast asleep. Beside him lay a little child, with her round white arms encircling his brown sinewy neck, and her golden-haired head resting upon the breast of his velveteen tunic. Her rosy lips were parted, showing the regular line of snow-white teeth within, and a playful smile played over her infantile features. Her plump little white legs, terminating in white socks and neat shoes with shining buckles, offered a strange contrast to the long shrivelled members of her companion. On the ledge of rock above this strange couple there stood three solemn buzzards, who, at the sight of the newcomers, uttered raucous screams of disappointment and flapped sullenly away.

The cries of the foul birds awoke the two sleepers, who stared about them in bewilderment. The man staggered to his feet and looked down upon the plain which had been so desolate when sleep had overtaken him, and which was now traversed by this enormous body of men and of beasts. His face assumed an expression of incredulity as he gazed, and he passed his bony hand over his eyes. 'This is what they call delirium, I guess,' he muttered. The child stood beside him, holding on to the skirt of his coat, and said nothing, but looked all around her with the wondering, questioning gaze of childhood.

The rescuing party were speedily able to convince the two castaways that their appearance was no delusion. One of them seized the little girl and hoisted her upon his shoulder, while two others supported her gaunt companion, and assisted him towards the wagons.

'My name is John Ferrier,' the wanderer explained; 'me and that little un are all that's left o' twenty-one people. The rest is all dead o' thirst and hunger away down in the south.'

'Is she your child?' asked someone.

'I guess she is now,' the other cried, defiantly; 'she's mine 'cause I saved her. No man will take her from me. She's Lucy Ferrier from this day on. Who are you though?' he continued, glancing with curiosity at his stalwart, sunburned rescuers; 'there seems to be a powerful lot of ye.'

'Nigh upon ten thousand,'[8] said one of the young men; 'we are the persecuted children of God – the chosen of the Angel Merona.'[9]

'I never heard tell on him,' said the wanderer. 'He appears to have chosen a fair crowd of ye.'

'Do not jest at that which is sacred,' said the other sternly. 'We are of those who believe in those sacred writings, drawn in Egyptian letters on plates of beaten gold, which were handed unto the holy Joseph Smith at Palmyra.[10] We have come from Nauvoo,[11] in the State of Illinois, where we had founded our temple. We have come to seek a refuge from the violent man and from the godless, even though it be the heart of the desert.'

The name of Nauvoo evidently recalled recollections to John Ferrier. 'I see,' he said, 'you are the Mormons.'

'We are the Mormons,'[12] answered his companions with one voice.

'And where are you going?'

'We do not know. The hand of God is leading us under the person of our Prophet. You must come before him. He shall say what is to be done with you.'

They had reached the base of the hill by this time, and were surrounded by crowds of the pilgrims – pale-faced, meek-looking women; strong, laughing children; and anxious earnest-eyed men. Many were the cries of astonishment and of commiseration which arose from them when they perceived the youth of one of the strangers and the destitution of the other. Their escort did not halt, however, but pushed on, followed by a great crowd of Mormons, until they reached a wagon, which was conspicuous for its great size and for the gaudiness and smartness of its appearance. Six horses were yoked to it, whereas the others were furnished with two, or, at most, four apiece. Beside the driver there sat a man who could not have been more than thirty years of age, but whose massive head and resolute expression marked him as leader. He was reading a brown-backed volume, but as the crowd approached he laid it aside, and listened attentively to an account of the episode. Then he turned to the two castaways.

'If we take you with us,' he said, in solemn words, 'it can only be as believers in our own creed. We shall have no wolves in our fold. Better far that your bones should bleach in this wilderness than that you should prove to be that little speck of decay which in time corrupts the whole fruit. Will you come with us on these terms?'

'Guess I'll come with you on any terms,' said Ferrier, with such emphasis that the grave Elders could not restrain a smile. The leader alone retained his stern, impressive expression.

'Take him, Brother Stangerson,' he said, 'give him food and drink, and the child likewise. Let it be your task also to teach him our holy creed. We have delayed long enough! Forward! On, on to Zion!'[13]

'On, on to Zion!' cried the crowd of Mormons, and the words rippled down the long caravan, passing from mouth to mouth until they died away in a dull murmur in the far distance. With a cracking of whips and a creaking of wheels the great wagons got into motion and soon the whole caravan was winding along once more. The Elder to whose care the two waifs had been committed led them to his wagon, where a meal was already awaiting them.

'You shall remain here,' he said. 'In a few days you will have recovered from your fatigues. In the meantime, remember that now and for ever you are of our religion. Brigham Young[14] has said it, and he has spoken with the voice of Joseph Smith, which is the voice of God.'

2

The Flower of Utah

This is not the place to commemorate the trials and privations endured by the immigrant Mormons before they came to their final haven. From the shores of the Mississippi to the western slopes of the Rocky Mountains they had struggled on with a constancy almost unparalleled in history. The savage man, and the savage beast, hunger, thirst, fatigue, and disease – every impediment which Nature could place in the way – had all been overcome with Anglo-Saxon tenacity. Yet the long journey and the accumulated terrors had shaken the hearts of the stoutest among them. There was not one who did not sink upon his knees in heartfelt prayer when they saw the broad valley of Utah bathed in the sunlight beneath them, and learned from the lips of their leader that this was the promised land, and that these virgin acres were to be theirs for evermore.

Young speedily proved himself to be a skilful administrator as well as a resolute chief. Maps were drawn and charts prepared, in which the future city was sketched out. All around farms were apportioned and allotted in proportion to the standing of each individual. The tradesman was put to his trade and the artisan to his calling. In the town streets and squares sprang up as if by magic. In the country there was draining and hedging, planting and clearing, until the next summer saw the whole country golden with the wheat crop. Everything prospered in the strange settlement. Above all, the great temple which they had erected in the centre of the city grew ever taller and larger. From the first blush of dawn until the closing of the twilight, the clatter of the hammer and the rasp of the saw were never absent from the monument which the immigrants erected to Him who had led them safe through many dangers.

The two castaways, John Ferrier and the little girl, who had shared his fortunes and had been adopted as his daughter, accompanied the Mormons to the end of their great pilgrimage. Little Lucy Ferrier was borne along pleasantly enough in Elder Stangerson's wagon, a retreat which she shared with the Mormon's three wives and with his son, a headstrong, forward boy of twelve. Having rallied, with the elasticity of childhood, from the shock caused by her mother's death, she soon became a pet with the women and reconciled herself to this new life in her moving canvas-covered home. In the meantime Ferrier having recovered from his privations, distinguished himself as a useful guide and an indefatigable hunter. So rapidly did he gain the esteem of his new companions, that when they reached the end of their wanderings, it was unanimously agreed that he should be provided with as large and as fertile a tract of land as any of the settlers, with the exception of Young himself, and of Stangerson, Kemball, Johnston, and Drebber, who were the four principal Elders.

On the farm thus acquired John Ferrier built himself a substantial log-house, which received so many additions in succeeding years that it grew into a roomy villa. He was a man of a practical turn of mind, keen in his dealings and skilful with his hands. His iron constitution enabled him to work morning and evening at improving and tilling his lands. Hence it came about that his farm and all that belonged to him prospered exceedingly. In three years he was better off than his neighbours, in six he was well-to-do, in nine he was rich, and in twelve there were not half a dozen men in the whole of Salt Lake City[1] who could compare with him. From the great inland sea[2] to the distant Wahsatch Mountains there was no name better known than that of John Ferrier.

There was one way and only one in which he offended the suscept-ibilities of his co-religionists. No argument or persuasion could ever induce him to set up a female establishment after the manner of his companions. He never gave reasons for this persistent refusal, but contented himself by resolutely and inflexibly adhering to his deter-mination. There were some who accused him of lukewarmness in his adopted religion, and others who put it down to greed of wealth and reluctance to incur expense. Others again spoke of some early love affair, and of a fair-haired girl who had pined away on the shores of the Atlantic. Whatever the reason, Ferrier remained strictly celibate. In every other respect he conformed to the religion of the young settlement, and gained the name of being an orthodox and straight-walking man.

Lucy Ferrier grew up within the log-house, and assisted her adopted father in all his undertakings. The keen air of the mountains and the balsamic odour of the pine trees took the place of nurse and mother to the young girl. As year succeeded to year she grew taller and stronger, her cheek more ruddy and her step more elastic. Many a wayfarer upon the high road which ran by Ferrier's farm felt long-forgotten thoughts revive in their minds as they watched her lithe, girlish figure tripping through the wheatfields, or met her mounted upon her father's mustang, and managing it with all the ease and grace of a true child of the West. So the bud blossomed into a flower, and the year which saw her father the richest of the farmers left her as fair a specimen of American girlhood as could be found in the whole Pacific slope.

It was not the father, however, who first discovered that the child had developed into the woman. It seldom is in such cases. That mysterious change is too subtle and too gradual to be measured by dates. Least of all does the maiden herself know it until the tone of a voice or the touch of a hand sets her heart thrilling within her, and she learns, with a mixture of pride and of fear, that a new and a larger nature has awoke within her. There are few who cannot recall that day and remember the one little incident which heralded the dawn of a new life. In the case of Lucy Ferrier the occasion was serious enough in itself, apart from its future influence on her destiny and that of many besides.

It was a warm June morning, and the Latter Day Saints[3] were as busy as the bees whose hive they have chosen for their emblem. In the fields and in the streets rose the same hum of human industry. Down the dusty high roads defiled long streams of heavily-laden mules, all heading to the west, for the gold fever[4] had broken out in California, and the overland route lay through the city of the Elect. There, too, were droves of sheep and bullocks coming in from the outlying pasture lands, and trains of tired immigrants, men and horses equally weary of their interminable journey. Through all this motley assemblage, threading her way with the skill of an accomplished rider, there galloped Lucy Ferrier, her fair face flushed with the exercise and her long chestnut hair floating out behind her. She had a commission from her father in the city, and was dashing in as she had done many a time before, with all the fearlessness of youth, thinking only of her task and how it was to be performed. The travel-stained adventurers gazed after her in astonishment, and even the unemotional Indians, journeying in with their peltries,[5] relaxed their accustomed stoicism as they marvelled at the beauty of the pale-faced maiden.

She had reached the outskirts of the city when she found the road blocked by a great drove of cattle, driven by a half-dozen wild-looking herdsmen from the plains. In her impatience she endeavoured to pass this obstacle by pushing her horse into what appeared to be a gap. Scarcely had she got fairly into it, however, before the beasts closed in behind her, and she found herself completely imbedded in the moving stream of fierce-eyed long-horned bullocks. Accustomed as she was to deal with cattle, she was not alarmed at her situation, but took advantage of every opportunity to urge her horse on, in the hopes of pushing her way through the cavalcade. Unfortunately the horns of one of the creatures, either by accident or design, came in violent contact with the flank of the mustang, and excited it to madness. In an instant it reared up upon its hind legs with a snort of rage, and pranced and tossed in a way that would have unseated any but a skilful rider. The situation was full of peril. Every plunge of the excited horse brought it against the horns again, and goaded it to fresh madness. It was all that the girl could do to keep herself in the saddle, yet a slip would mean a terrible death under the hoofs of the unwieldy and terrified animals. Unaccustomed to sudden emergencies, her head began to swim, and her grip upon the bridle to relax. Choked by the rising cloud of dust and by the steam from the struggling creatures, she might have abandoned her efforts in despair, but for a kindly voice at her elbow which assured her of assistance. At the same moment a sinewy brown hand caught the frightened horse by the curb, and forcing a way through the drove, soon brought her to the outskirts.

'You're not hurt, I hope, miss,' said her preserver, respectfully.

She looked up at his dark, fierce face, and laughed saucily. 'I'm awful frightened,' she said, naïvely; 'whoever would have thought that Poncho[6] would have been so scared by a lot of cows?'

'Thank God you kept your seat,' the other said earnestly. He was a tall, savage-looking young fellow, mounted on a powerful roan horse, and clad in the rough dress of a hunter, with a long rifle slung over his shoulders. 'I guess you are the daughter of John Ferrier,' he remarked; 'I saw you ride down from his house. When you see him, ask him if he remembers the Jefferson Hopes of St Louis.[7] If he's the same Ferrier, my father and he were pretty thick.'

'Hadn't you better come and ask yourself?' she asked, demurely.

The young fellow seemed pleased at the suggestion, and his dark eyes sparkled with pleasure. 'I'll do so,' he said; 'we've been in the mountains for two months, and are not over and above in visiting condition. He must take us as he finds us.'

'He has a good deal to thank you for, and so have I,' she answered, 'he's awful fond of me. If those cows had jumped on me he'd have never got over it.'

'Neither would I,' said her companion.

'You! Well, I don't see that it would make much matter to you, anyhow. You ain't even a friend of ours.'

The young hunter's dark face grew so gloomy over this remark that Lucy Ferrier laughed aloud.

'There, I didn't mean that,' she said; 'of course, you are a friend now. You must come and see us. Now I must push along, or father won't trust me with his business any more. Good-bye!'

'Good-bye,' he answered, raising his broad sombrero, and bending over her little hand. She wheeled her mustang round, gave it a cut with her riding-whip, and darted away down the broad road in a rolling cloud of dust.

Young Jefferson Hope rode on with his companions, gloomy and taciturn. He and they had been among the Nevada Mountains prospecting for silver, and were returning to Salt Lake City in the hope of raising capital enough to work some lodes which they had discovered. He had been as keen as any of them upon the business until this sudden incident had drawn his thoughts into another channel. The sight of the fair young girl, as frank and wholesome as the Sierra breezes, had stirred his volcanic, untamed heart to its depths. When she had vanished from his sight, he realized that a crisis had come in his life, and that neither silver speculations nor any other questions could ever be of such importance to him as this new and all-absorbing one. The love which had sprung up in his heart was not the sudden, changeable fancy of a boy, but rather that wild, fierce passion of a man of strong will and imperious temper. He had been accustomed to succeed in all that he undertook. He swore in his heart that he would not fail in this if human effort and human perseverance could render him successful.

He called on John Ferrier that night, and many times again, until his face was a familiar one at the farmhouse. John, cooped up in the valley, and absorbed in his work, had had little chance of learning the news of the outside world during the last twelve years. All this Jefferson Hope was able to tell him, and in a style which interested Lucy as well as her father. He had been a pioneer in California, and could narrate many a strange tale of fortunes made and fortunes lost in those wild, halcyon days. He had been a scout, too, and a trapper, a silver explorer, and a ranch-man. Wherever stirring adventures were to be had, Jefferson Hope had been there in search of them. He soon became a favourite with the old farmer, who spoke eloquently of his virtues. On such occasions, Lucy was silent, but her blushing cheek and her bright, happy eyes showed only too clearly that her young heart was no longer her own. Her honest father may not have observed these symptoms, but they were assuredly not thrown away upon the man who had won her affections.

One summer evening he came galloping down the road and pulled up at the gate. She was at the doorway, and came down to meet him. He threw the bridle over the fence and strode up the pathway.

'I am off, Lucy,' he said, taking her two hands in his, and gazing tenderly down into her face; 'I won't ask you to come with me now, but will you be ready to come when I am here again?'

'And when will that be?' she asked, blushing and laughing.

'A couple of months at the outside. I will come and claim you then, my darling. There's no one who can stand between us.'

'And how about Father?' she asked.

'He has given his consent, provided we get these mines working all right. I have no fear on that head.'

'Oh, well; of course, if you and Father have arranged it all, there's no more to be said,' she whispered, with her cheek against his broad breast.

'Thank God!' he said, hoarsely, stooping and kissing her. 'It is settled, then. The longer I stay, the harder it will be to go. They are waiting for me at the canyon. Good-bye, my own darling – good-bye. In two months you shall see me.'

He tore himself from her as he spoke, and, flinging himself upon his horse, galloped furiously away, never even looking round, as though afraid that his resolution might fail him if he took one glance at what he was leaving. She stood at the gate, gazing after him until he vanished from her sight. Then she walked back into the house, the happiest girl in all Utah.

3

John Ferrier Talks with the Prophet

Three weeks had passed since Jefferson Hope and his comrades had departed from Salt Lake City. John Ferrier's heart was sore within him when he thought of the young man's return, and of the impending loss of his adopted child. Yet her bright and happy face reconciled him to the arrangement more than any argument could have done. He had always determined, deep down in his resolute heart, that nothing would ever induce him to allow his daughter to wed a Mormon. Such a marriage he regarded as no marriage at all, but as a shame and a disgrace. Whatever he might think of the Mormon doctrines, upon that one point he was inflexible. He had to seal his mouth on the subject, however, for to express an unorthodox opinion was a dangerous matter in those days in the Land of the Saints.

Yes, a dangerous matter – so dangerous that even the most saintly dared only whisper their religious opinions with bated breath, lest something which fell from their lips might be misconstrued, and bring down a swift retribution upon them. The victims of persecution had now turned persecutors on their own account and persecutors of the most terrible description. Not the Inquisition of Seville, nor the German Vehmgericht, nor the Secret Societies of Italy, were ever able to put a more formidable machinery in motion than that which cast a cloud over the State of Utah.

Its invisibility, and the mystery which was attached to it, made this organization doubly terrible. It appeared to be omniscient and omnipotent, and yet was neither seen nor heard. The man who held out against the Church vanished away, and none knew whither he had gone or what had befallen him. His wife and his children awaited him at home, but no father ever returned to tell them how he had fared at the hands of his secret judges. A rash word or a hasty act was followed by annihilation, and yet none knew what the nature might be of this terrible power which was suspended over them. No wonder that men went about in fear and trembling, and that even in the heart of the wilderness they dared not whisper the doubts which oppressed them.

At first this vague and terrible power was exercised only upon the recalcitrants who, having embraced the Mormon faith, wished afterwards to pervert or to abandon it. Soon, however, it took a wider range. The supply of adult women was running short, and polygamy without a female population on which to draw was a barren doctrine indeed. Strange rumours began to be bandied about – rumours of murdered immigrants and rifled camps in regions where Indians had never been seen. Fresh women appeared in the harems of the Elders – women who pined and wept, and bore upon their faces the traces of an unextinguishable horror. Belated wanderers upon the mountains spoke of gangs of armed men, masked, stealthy, and noiseless, who flitted by them in the darkness. These tales and rumours took substance and shape, and were corroborated and recorroborated, until they resolved themselves into a definite name. To this day, in the lonely ranches of the West, the name of the Danite Band,[1] or the Avenging Angels, is a sinister and an ill-omened one.

Fuller knowledge of the organization which produced such terrible results served to increase rather than to lessen the horror which it inspired in the minds of men. None knew who belonged to this ruthless society. The names of the participators in the deeds of blood and violence done under the name of religion were kept profoundly secret. The very friend to whom you communicated your misgivings as to the Prophet and his mission might be one of those who would come forth at night with fire and sword to exact a terrible reparation. Hence every man feared his neighbour, and none spoke of the things which were nearest his heart.

One fine morning John Ferrier was about to set out to his wheatfields, when he heard the click of the latch, and, looking through the window, saw a stout, sandy-haired middle-aged man coming up the pathway. His heart leapt to his mouth, for this was none other than the great Brigham Young himself. Full of trepidation – for he knew that such a visit boded him little good – Ferrier ran to the door to greet the Mormon chief. The latter, however, received his salutations coldly, and followed him with a stern face into the sitting-room.

'Brother Ferrier,' he said, taking a seat, and eyeing the farmer keenly from under his light-coloured eyelashes, 'the true believers have been good friends to you. We picked you up when you were starving in the desert, we shared our food with you, led you safe to the Chosen Valley, gave you a goodly share of land, and allowed you to wax rich under our protection. Is not this so?'

'It is so,' answered John Ferrier.

'In return for all this we asked but one condition: that was, that you should embrace the true faith, and conform in every way to its usages. This you promised to do, and this, if common report says truly, you have neglected.'

'And how have I neglected it?' asked Ferrier, throwing out his hands in expostulation. 'Have I not given to the common fund? Have I not attended at the Temple? Have I not –?'

'Where are your wives?' asked Young, looking round him. 'Call them in, that I may greet them.'

'It is true that I have not married,' Ferrier answered. 'But women were few, and there were many who had better claims than I. I was not a lonely man: I had my daughter to attend to my wants.'

'It is of that daughter that I would speak to you,' said the leader of the Mormons. 'She has grown to be the flower of Utah, and has found favour in the eyes of many who are high in the land.'

John Ferrier groaned inwardly.

'There are stories of her which I would fain disbelieve – stories that she is sealed to some Gentile.² This must be the gossip of idle tongues.

'What is the thirteenth rule in the code of the sainted Joseph Smith? "Let every maiden of the true faith marry one of the elect; for if she wed a Gentile, she commits a grievous sin." This being so, it is impossible that you, who profess the holy creed, should suffer your daughter to violate it.'

John Ferrier made no answer, but he played nervously with his riding-whip.

'Upon this one point your whole faith shall be tested – so it has been decided in the Sacred Council of Four. The girl is young, and we would not have her wed grey hairs, neither would we deprive her of all choice. We Elders have many heifers,[3] but our children must also be provided. Stangerson has a son, and Drebber has a son, and either of them would gladly welcome your daughter to their house. Let her choose between them. They are young and rich, and of the true faith. What say you to that?'

Ferrier remained silent for some little time with his brows knitted.

'You will give us time,' he said at last. 'My daughter is very young – she is scarce of an age to marry.'

'She shall have a month to choose,' said Young, rising from his seat. 'At the end of that time she shall give her answer.'

He was passing through the door, when he turned, with flushed face and flashing eyes. 'It were better for you, John Ferrier,' he thundered, 'that you and she were now lying blanched skeletons upon the Sierra Blanco, than that you should put your weak wills against the orders of the Holy Four!'

With a threatening gesture of his hand, he turned from the door, and Ferrier heard his heavy steps scrunching along the shingly path.

He was still sitting with his elbow upon his knee considering how he should broach the matter to his daughter, when a soft hand was laid upon his, and looking up, he saw her standing beside him. One glance at her pale, frightened face showed him that she had heard what had passed.

'I could not help it,' she said, in answer to his look. 'His voice rang through the house. Oh, Father, Father, what shall we do?'

'Don't you scare yourself,' he answered, drawing her to him, and passing his broad, rough hand caressingly over her chestnut hair. 'We'll fix it up somehow or another. You don't find your fancy kind o' lessening for this chap, do you?'

A sob and a squeeze of his hand was her only answer.

'No; of course not. I shouldn't care to hear you say you did. He's a likely lad, and he's a Christian, which is more than these folk here, in spite o' all their praying and preaching. There's a party starting for Nevada tomorrow, and I'll manage to send him a message letting him know the hole we are in. If I know anything o' that young man, he'll be back here with a speed that would whip electro-telegraphs.'

Lucy laughed through her tears at her father's description.

'When he comes, he will advise us for the best. But it is for you that I am frightened, dear. One hears – one hears such dreadful stories about those who oppose the Prophet: something terrible always happens to them.'

'But we haven't opposed him yet,' her father answered. 'It will be time to look out for squalls when we do. We have a clear month before us; at the end of that, I guess we had best shin out of Utah.'

'Leave Utah!'

'That's about the size of it.'

'But the farm?'

'We will raise as much as we can in money, and let the rest go. To tell the truth, Lucy, it isn't the first time I have thought of doing it. I don't care about knuckling under to any man, as these folk do to their darned Prophet. I'm a free-born American, and it's all new to me. Guess I'm too old to learn. If he comes browsing about this farm, he might chance to run up against a charge of buck-shot travelling in the opposite direction.'

'But they won't let us leave,' his daughter objected.

'Wait till Jefferson comes, and we'll soon manage that. In the meantime, don't you fret yourself, my dearie, and don't get your eyes swelled up, else he'll be walking into me when he sees you. There's nothing to be afeard about, and there's no danger at all.'

John Ferrier uttered these consoling remarks in a very confident tone, but she could not help observing that he paid unusual care to the fastening of the doors that night, and that he carefully cleaned and loaded the rusty old shot-gun which hung upon the wall of his bedroom.

4

A Flight for Life

On the morning which followed his interview with the Mormon Prophet, John Ferrier went in to Salt Lake City, and having found his acquaintance, who was bound for the Nevada Mountains, he entrusted him with his message to Jefferson Hope. In it he told the young man of the imminent danger which threatened them, and how necessary it was that he should return. Having done thus he felt easier in his mind, and returned home with a lighter heart.

As he approached his farm, he was surprised to see a horse hitched to each of the posts of the gate. Still more surprised was he on entering to find two young men in possession of his sitting-room. One, with a long pale face, was leaning back in the rocking-chair, with his feet cocked up upon the stove. The other, a bull-necked youth with coarse, bloated features, was standing in front of the window with his hands in his pockets whistling a popular hymn. Both of them nodded to Ferrier as he entered, and the one in the rocking-chair commenced the conversation.

'Maybe you don't know us,' he said. 'This here is the son of Elder Drebber, and I'm Joseph Stangerson, who travelled with you in the desert when the Lord stretched out His hand and gathered you into the true fold.'

'As He will all the nations in His own good time,' said the other in a nasal voice; 'He grindeth slowly but exceedingly small.'

John Ferrier bowed coldly. He had guessed who his visitors were.

'We have come,' continued Stangerson, 'at the advice of our fathers to solicit the hand of your daughter for whichever of us may seem good to you and to her. As I have but four wives and Brother Drebber here has seven, it appears to me that my claim is the stronger one.'

'Nay, nay, Brother Stangerson,' cried the other; 'the question is not now many wives we have, but how many we can keep. My father has now given over his mills to me, and I am the richer man.'

'But my prospects are better,' said the other, warmly. 'When the Lord removes my father, I shall have his tanning yard and his leather factory. Then I am your elder, and am higher in the Church.'

'It will be for the maiden to decide,' rejoined young Drebber, smirking at his own reflection in the glass. 'We will leave it all to her decision.'

During this dialogue John Ferrier had stood fuming in the doorway, hardly able to keep his riding-whip from the backs of his two visitors.

'Look here,' he said at last, striding up to them, 'when my daughter summons you, you can come, but until then I don't want to see your faces again.'

The two young Mormons stared at him in amazement. In their eyes this competition between them for the maiden's hand was the highest of honours both to her and her father.

'There are two ways out of the room,' cried Ferrier; 'there is the door, and there is the window. Which do you care to use?'

His brown face looked so savage, and his gaunt hands so threatening, that his visitors sprang to their feet and beat a hurried retreat. The old farmer followed them to the door.

'Let me know when you have settled which it is to be,' he said, sardonically.

'You shall smart for this!'[1] Stangerson cried, white with rage. 'You have defied the Prophet and the Council of Four. You shall rue it to the end of your days.'

'The hand of the Lord shall be heavy upon you,' cried young Drebber; 'He will arise and smite you!'

'Then I'll start the smiting,' exclaimed Ferrier, furiously, and would have rushed upstairs for his gun had not Lucy seized him by the arm and restrained him. Before he could escape from her, the clatter of horses' hoofs told him that they were beyond his reach.

'The young canting rascals!' he exclaimed, wiping the perspiration from his forehead; 'I would sooner see you in your grave, my girl, than the wife of either of them.'

'And so should I, Father,' she answered, with spirit; 'but Jefferson will soon be here.'

'Yes. It will not be long before he comes. The sooner the better, for we do not know what their next move may be.'

It was, indeed, high time that someone capable of giving advice and help should come to the aid of the sturdy old farmer and his adopted daughter. In the whole history of the settlement there had never been such a case of rank disobedience to the authority of the Elders. If minor errors were punished so sternly, what would be the fate of this arch rebel? Ferrier knew that his wealth and position would be of no avail to him. Others as well known and as rich as himself had been spirited away before now, and their goods given over to the Church. He was a brave man, but he trembled at the vague, shadowy terrors which hung over him. Any known danger he could face with a firm lip, but this suspense was unnerving. He concealed his fears from his daughter, however, and affected to make light of the whole matter, though she, with the keen eye of love, saw plainly that he was ill at ease.

He expected that he would receive some message or remonstrance from Young as to his conduct, and he was not mistaken, though it came in an unlooked-for manner. Upon rising next morning he found, to his surprise, a small square of paper pinned on to the coverlet of his bed just over his chest. On it was printed, in bold, straggling letters:

'Twenty-nine days are given you for amendment, and then – '

The dash was more fear-inspiring than any threat could have been. How this warning came into his room puzzled John Ferrier surely, for his servants slept in an outhouse, and the doors and windows had all been secured. He crumpled the paper up and said nothing to his daughter, but the incident struck a chill into his heart. The twenty-nine days were evidently the balance of the month which Young had promised. What strength or courage could avail against an enemy armed with such mysterious powers? The hand which fastened that pin might have struck him to the heart, and he could never have known who had slain him.

Still more shaken was he next morning. They had sat down to their breakfast, when Lucy with a cry of surprise pointed upwards. In the centre of the ceiling was scrawled, with a burned stick apparently, the number 28. To his daughter it was unintelligible, and he did not enlighten her. That night he sat up with his gun and kept watch and ward. He saw and he heard nothing, and yet in the morning a great 27 had been painted upon the outside of his door.

Thus day followed day; and as sure as morning came he found that his unseen enemies had kept their register, and had marked up in some conspicuous position how many days were still left to him out of the month of grace. Sometimes the fatal numbers appeared upon the walls, sometimes upon the floors, occasionally they were on small placards stuck upon the garden gate or the railings. With all his vigilance John Ferrier could not discover whence these daily warnings proceeded. A horror which was almost superstitious came upon him at the sight of them. He became haggard and restless, and his eyes had the troubled look of some hunted creature. He had but one hope in life now, and that was for the arrival of the young hunter from Nevada.

Twenty had changed to fifteen, and fifteen to ten, but there was no news of the absentee. One by one the numbers dwindled down, and still there came no sign of him. Whenever a horseman clattered down the road, or a driver shouted at his team, the old farmer hurried to the gate, thinking that help had arrived at last. At last, when he saw five give way to four and that again to three, he lost heart, and abandoned all hope of escape. Single-handed, and with his limited knowledge of the mountains which surrounded the settlement, he knew that he was powerless. The more frequented roads were strictly watched and guarded, and none could pass along them without an order from the Council. Turn which way he would, there appeared to be no avoiding the blow which hung over him. Yet the old man never wavered in his resolution to part with life itself before he consented to what he regarded as his daughter's dishonour.

He was sitting alone one evening pondering deeply over his troubles, and searching vainly for some way out of them. That morning had shown the figure 2 upon the wall of his house, and the next day would be the last of the allotted time. What was to happen then? All manner of vague and terrible fancies filled his imagination. And his daughter – what was to become of her after he was gone? Was there no escape from the invisible network which was drawn all round them? He sank his head upon the table and sobbed at the thought of his own impotence.

What was that? In the silence he heard a gentle scratching sound – low, but very distinct in the quiet of the night. It came from the door of the house. Ferrier crept into the hall and listened intently. There was a pause for a few moments, and then the low, insidious sound was repeated. Someone was evidently tapping very gently upon one of the panels of the door. Was it some midnight assassin who had come to carry out the murderous orders of the secret tribunal? Or was it some agent who was marking up that the last day of grace had arrived? John Ferrier felt that instant death would be better than the suspense which shook his nerves and chilled his heart. Springing forward, he drew the bolt and threw the door open.

Outside all was calm and quiet. The night was fine, and the stars were twinkling brightly overhead. The little front garden lay before the farmer's eyes bounded by the fence and gate, but neither there nor on the road was any human being to be seen. With a sigh of relief, Ferrier looked to right and to left, until, happening to glance straight down at his own feet, he saw to his astonishment a man lying flat upon his face upon the ground, with arms and legs all asprawl.

So unnerved was he at the sight that he leaned up against the wall with his hand to his throat to stifle his inclination to call out. His first thought was that the prostrate figure was that of some wounded or dying man, but as he watched it he saw it writhe along the ground and into the hall with the rapidity and noiselessness of a serpent. Once within the house the man sprang to his feet, closed the door, and revealed to the astonished farmer the fierce face and resolute expression of Jefferson Hope.

'Good God!' gasped John Ferrier. 'How you scared me. Whatever made you come in like that?'

'Give me food,' the other said hoarsely. 'I have had no time for bite or sup for eight-and-forty hours.' He flung himself upon the cold meat and bread which were still lying upon the table from his host's supper, and devoured it voraciously. 'Does Lucy bear up well?' he asked, when he had satisfied his hunger.

'Yes. She does not know the danger,' her father answered.

'That is well. The house is watched on every side. That is why I crawled my way up to it. They may be darned sharp, but they're not quite sharp enough to catch a Washoe hunter.'

John Ferrier felt a different man now that he realized that he had a devoted ally. He seized the young man's leathery hand and wrung it cordially. 'You're a man to be proud of,' he said. 'There are not many who would come to share our danger and our troubles.'

'You've hit it there, pard,' the young hunter answered. 'I have a respect for you, but if you were alone in this business I'd think twice before I put my head into such a hornets' nest. It's Lucy that brings me here, and before harm comes on her I guess there will be one less o' the Hope family in Utah.'

'What are we to do?'

'Tomorrow is your last day, and unless you act tonight you are lost. I have a mule and two horses waiting in the Eagle Ravine. How much money have you?'

'Two thousand dollars in gold and five in notes.'

'That will do. I have as much more to add to it. We must push for Carson City[2] through the mountains. You had best wake Lucy. It is as well that the servants do not sleep in the house.'

While Ferrier was absent, preparing his daughter for the approaching journey Jefferson Hope packed all the eatables that he could find into a small parcel, and filled a stoneware jar with water, for he knew by experience that the mountain wells were few and far between. He had hardly completed his arrangements before the farmer returned with his daughter all dressed and ready for a start. The greeting between the lovers was warm, but brief for minutes were precious, and there was much to be done.

'We must make our start at once,' said Jefferson Hope, speaking in a low but resolute voice, like one who realizes the greatness of the peril, but has steeled his heart to meet it. 'The front and back entrances are watched, but with caution we may get away through the side window and across the fields. Once on the road we are only two miles from the Ravine where the horses are waiting. By daybreak we should be halfway through the mountains.'

'What if we are stopped?' asked Ferrier.

Hope slapped the revolver butt which protruded from the front of his tunic. 'If they are too many for us, we shall take two or three of them with us,' he said with a sinister smile.

The lights inside the house had all been extinguished, and from the darkened window Ferrier peered over the fields which had been his own, and which he was now about to abandon for ever. He had long nerved himself to the sacrifice, however, and the thought of the honour and happiness of his daughter out-weighed any regret at his ruined fortunes. All looked so peaceful and happy, the rustling trees and the broad silent stretch of grainland, that it was difficult to realize that the spirit of murder lurked through it all. Yet the white face and set expression of the young hunter showed that in his approach to the house he had seen enough to satisfy him upon that head.

Ferrier carried the bag of gold and notes. Jefferson Hope had the scanty provisions and water, while Lucy had a small bundle containing a few of her more valued possessions. Opening the window very slowly and carefully, they waited until a dark cloud had somewhat obscured the night, and then one by one passed through into the little garden. With bated breath and crouching figures they stumbled across it, and gained the shelter of the hedge, which they skirted until they came to the gap which opened into the cornfield. They had just reached this point when the young man seized his two companions and dragged them down into the shadow, where they lay silent and trembling.

It was as well that his prairie training had given Jefferson Hope the ears of a lynx. He and his friends had hardly crouched down before the melancholy hooting of a mountain owl was heard within a few yards of them, which was immediately answered by another hoot at a small distance. At the same moment a vague, shadowy figure emerged from the gap for which they had been making, and uttered the plaintive signal cry again, on which a second man appeared out of the obscurity.

'Tomorrow at midnight,' said the first, who appeared to be in authority. 'When the Whip-poor-Will calls three times.'

'It is well,' returned the other. 'Shall I tell Brother Drebber?'

'Pass it on to him, and from him to the others. Nine to seven!'

'Seven to five!' repeated the other; and the two figures flitted away in different directions. Their concluding words had evidently been some form of sign and countersign. The instant that their footsteps had died away in the distance, Jefferson Hope sprang to his feet, and helping his companions through the gap, led the way across the fields at the top of his speed, supporting and half-carrying the girl when her strength appeared to fail her.

'Hurry on! hurry on!' he gasped from time to time. 'We are through the line of sentinels. Everything depends on speed. Hurry on!'

Once on the high road, they made rapid progress. Only once did they meet anyone, and then they managed to slip into a field, and so avoid recognition. Before reaching the town the hunter branched away into a rugged and narrow footpath which led to the mountains. Two dark, jagged peaks loomed above them through the darkness, and the defile which led between them was the Eagle Canyon in which the horses were awaiting them. With unerring instinct Jefferson Hope picked his way among the great boulders and along the bed of a dried-up water-course, until he came to the retired corner screened with rocks, where the faithful animals had been picketed. The girl was placed upon the mule, and old Ferrier upon one of the horses, with his money-bag, while Jefferson Hope led the other along the precipitous and dangerous path.

It was a bewildering route for anyone who was not accustomed to face Nature in her wildest moods. On the one side a great crag towered up a thousand feet or more, black, stern, and menacing, with long basaltic columns upon its rugged surface like the ribs of some petrified monster. On the other hand a wild chaos of boulders and debris made all advance impossible. Between the two ran the irregular track, so narrow in places that they had to travel in Indian file, and so rough that only practised riders could have traversed it at all. Yet, in spite of all dangers and difficulties, the hearts of the fugitives were light within them, for every step increased the distance between them and the terrible despotism from which they were flying.

They soon had a proof, however, that they were still within the jurisdiction of the Saints. They had reached the very wildest and most desolate portion of the pass when the girl gave a startled cry, and pointed upwards. On a rock which overlooked the track, showing out dark and plain against the sky, there stood a solitary sentinel. He saw them as soon as they perceived him, and his military challenge of 'Who goes there?' rang through the silent ravine.

'Travellers for Nevada,' said Jefferson Hope, with his hand upon the rifle which hung by his saddle.

They could see the lonely watcher fingering his gun, and peering down at them as if dissatisfied at their reply.

'By whose permission?' he asked.

'The Holy Four,' answered Ferrier. His Mormon experiences had taught him that that was the highest authority to which he could refer.

'Nine to seven,' cried the sentinel.

'Seven to five,' returned Jefferson Hope promptly, remembering the countersign which he had heard in the garden.

'Pass, and the Lord go with you,' said the voice from above. Beyond his post the path broadened out, and the horses were able to break into a trot. Looking back, they could see the solitary watcher leaning upon his gun, and knew that they had passed the outlying post of the chosen people, and that freedom lay before them.

5

The Avenging Angels

All night their course lay through intricate defiles and over irregular and rock-strewn paths. More than once they lost their way, but Hope's intimate knowledge of the mountains enabled them to regain the track once more. When morning broke a scene of marvellous though savage beauty lay before them. In every direction the great snow-capped peaks hemmed them in, peeping over each other's shoulders to the far horizon. So steep were the rocky banks on either side of them that the larch and the pine seemed to be suspended over their heads, and to need only a gust of wind to come hurtling down upon them. Nor was the fear entirely an illusion, for the barren valley was thickly strewn with trees and boulders which had fallen in a similar manner. Even as they passed, a great rock came thundering down with a hoarse rattle which woke the echoes in the silent gorges, and startled the weary horses into a gallop.

As the sun rose slowly above the eastern horizon, the caps of the great mountains lit up one after the other, like lamps at a festival, until they were all ruddy and glowing. The magnificent spectacle cheered the hearts of the three fugitives and gave them fresh energy. At a wild torrent which swept out of a ravine they called a halt and watered their horses, while they partook of a hasty breakfast. Lucy and her father would fain have rested longer, but Jefferson Hope was inexorable. 'They will be upon our track by this time,' he said. 'Everything depends upon our speed. Once safe in Carson, we may rest for the remainder of our lives.'

During the whole of that day they struggled on through the defiles, and by evening they calculated that they were more than thirty miles from their enemies. At night-time they chose the base of a beetling crag, where the rocks offered some protection from the chill wind, and there, huddled together for warmth, they enjoyed a few hours' sleep. Before daybreak, however, they were up and on their way once more. They had seen no signs of any pursuers, and Jefferson Hope began to think that they were fairly out of the reach of the terrible organization whose enmity they had incurred. He little knew how far that iron grasp could reach, or how soon it was to close upon them and crush them.

About the middle of the second day of their flight their scanty store of provisions began to run out. This gave the hunter little uneasiness, however, for there was game to be had among the mountains, and he had frequently before had to depend upon his rifle for the needs of life. Choosing a sheltered nook, he piled together a few dried branches and made a blazing fire, at which his companions might warm themselves, for they were now nearly five thousand feet above the sea level, and the air was bitter and keen. Having tethered the horses, and bade Lucy adieu, he threw his gun over his shoulder, and set out in search of whatever chance might throw in his way. Looking back, he saw the old man and the young girl crouching over the blazing fire, while the three animals stood motionless in the background. Then the intervening rocks hid them from his view.

He walked for a couple of miles through one ravine after another without success, though, from the marks upon the bark of the trees, and other indications, he judged that there were numerous bears in the vicinity. At last, after two or three hours' fruitless search, he was thinking of turning back in despair, when casting his eyes upwards he saw a sight which sent a thrill of pleasure through his heart. On the edge of a jutting pinnacle, three or four hundred feet above him, there stood a creature somewhat resembling a sheep in appearance, but armed with a pair of gigantic horns. The big-horn – for so it is called – was acting, probably, as a guardian over a flock which were invisible to the hunter; but fortunately it was heading in the opposite direction, and had not perceived him. Lying on his face, he rested his rifle upon a rock, and took a long and steady aim before drawing the trigger. The animal sprang into the air, tottered for a moment upon the edge of the precipice, and then came crashing down into the valley beneath.

The creature was too unwieldy to lift, so the hunter contented himself with cutting away one haunch and part of the flank. With this trophy over his shoulder, he hastened to retrace his steps, for the evening was already drawing in. He had hardly started, however, before he realized the difficulty which faced him. In his eagerness he had wandered far past the ravines which were known to him, and it was no easy matter to pick out the path which he had taken. The valley in which he found himself divided and subdivided into many gorges, which were so like each other that it was impossible to distinguish one from the other. He followed one for a mile or more until he came to a mountain torrent which he was sure that he had never seen before. Convinced that he had taken the wrong turn, he tried another, but with the same result. Night was coming on rapidly, and it was almost dark before he at last found himself in a defile which was familiar to him. Even then it was no easy matter to keep to the right track, for the moon had not yet risen, and the high cliffs on either side made the obscurity more profound. Weighed down with his burden, and weary from his exertions, he stumbled along, keeping up his heart by the reflection that every step brought him nearer to Lucy, and that he carried with him enough to ensure them food for the remainder of their journey.

He had now come to the mouth of the very defile in which he had left them. Even in the darkness he could recognize the outline of the cliffs which bounded it. They must, he reflected, be awaiting him anxiously, for he had been absent nearly five hours. In the gladness of his heart he put his hands to his mouth and made the glen re-echo to a loud halloo as a signal that he was coming. He paused and listened for an answer. None came save his own cry, which clattered up the dreary, silent ravines, and was borne back to his ears in countless repetitions. Again he shouted, even louder than before, and again no whisper came back from the friends whom he had left such a short time ago. A vague, nameless dread came over him, and he hurried onwards frantically, dropping the precious food in his agitation.

When he turned the corner, he came full in sight of the spot where the fire had been lit. There was still a glowing pile of wood ashes there, but it had evidently not been tended since his departure. The same dead silence still reigned all round. With his fears all changed to convictions, he hurried on. There was no living creature near the remains of the fire: animals, man, maiden, all were gone. It was only too clear that some sudden and terrible disaster had occurred during his absence – a disaster which had embraced them all, and yet had left no traces behind it.

Bewildered and stunned by this blow, Jefferson Hope felt his head spin round, and had to lean upon his rifle to save himself from falling. He was essentially a man of action, however, and speedily recovered from his temporary impotence. Seizing a half-consumed piece of wood from the smouldering fire, he blew it into a flame, and proceeded with its help to examine the little camp. The ground was all stamped down by the feet of horses, showing that a large party of mounted men had overtaken the fugitives, and the direction of their tracks proved that they had afterwards turned back to Salt Lake City. Had they carried back both of his companions with them? Jefferson Hope had almost persuaded himself that they must have done so, when his eye fell upon an object which made every nerve of his body tingle within him. A little way on one side of the camp was a low-lying heap of reddish soil, which had assuredly not been there before. There was no mistaking it for anything but a newly-dug grave. As the young hunter approached it, he perceived that a stick had been planted on it, with a sheet of paper stuck in the cleft fork of it. The inscription upon the paper was brief, but to the point:

JOHN FERRIER
Formerly of Salt Lake City
Died August 4th, 1860

The sturdy old man, whom he had left so short a time before, was gone, then, and this was all his epitaph. Jefferson Hope looked wildly round to see if there was a second grave, but there was no sign of one. Lucy had been carried back by their terrible pursuers to fulfil her original destiny, by becoming one of the harem of the Elder's son. As the young fellow realized the certainty of her fate, and his own powerlessness to prevent it, he wished that he, too, was lying with the old farmer in his last silent resting-place.

Again, however, his active spirit shook off the lethargy which springs from despair. If there was nothing else left to him, he could at least devote his life to revenge. With indomitable patience and perseverance, Jefferson Hope possessed also a power of sustained vindictiveness, which he may have learned from the Indians amongst whom he had lived. As he stood by the desolate fire, he felt that the only one thing which could assuage his grief would be thorough and complete retribution, brought by his own hand upon his enemies. His strong will and untiring energy should, he determined, be devoted to that one end. With a grim, white face, he retraced his steps to where he had dropped the food, and having stirred up the smouldering fire, he cooked enough to last him for a few days. This he made up into a bundle, and, tired as he was, he set himself to walk back through the mountains upon the track of the Avenging Angels.

For five days he toiled footsore and weary through the defiles which he had already traversed on horseback. At night he flung himself down among the rocks, and snatched a few hours of sleep; but before daybreak he was always well on his way. On the sixth day, he reached the Eagle Canyon, from which they had commenced their ill-fated flight. Thence he could look down upon the home of the Saints. Worn and exhausted, he leaned upon his rifle and shook his gaunt hand fiercely at the silent widespread city beneath him. As he looked at it, he observed that there were flags in some of the principal streets, and other signs of festivity. He was still speculating as to what this might mean when he heard the clatter of horse's hoofs, and saw a mounted man riding towards him. As he approached, he recognized him as a Mormon named Cowper, to whom he had rendered services at different times. He therefore accosted him when he got up to him, with the object of finding out what Lucy Ferrier's fate had been.

'I am Jefferson Hope,' he said. 'You remember me.'

The Mormon looked at him with undisguised astonishment – indeed, it was difficult to recognize in this tattered, unkempt wanderer, with ghastly white face and fierce, wild eyes, the spruce young hunter of former days. Having, however, at last satisfied himself as to his identity, the man's surprise changed to consternation.

'You are mad to come here,' he cried. 'It is as much as my own life is worth to be seen talking with you. There is a warrant against you from the Holy Four for assisting the Ferriers away.'

'I don't fear them, or their warrant,' Hope said, earnestly. 'You must know something of this matter, Cowper. I conjure you by everything you hold dear to answer a few questions. We have always been friends. For God's sake, don't refuse to answer me.'

'What is it?' the Mormon asked uneasily. 'Be quick. The very rocks have ears and the trees eyes.'

'What has become of Lucy Ferrier?'

'She was married yesterday to young Drebber. Hold up, man, hold up; you have no life left in you.'

'Don't mind me,' said Hope faintly. He was white to the very lips, and had sunk down on the stone against which he had been leaning. 'Married, you say?'

'Married yesterday – that's what those flags are for on the Endowment House. There was some words between young Drebber and young Stangerson as to which was to have her. They'd both been in the party that followed them, and Stangerson had shot her father, which seemed to give him the best claim; but when they argued it out in council, Drebber's party was the stronger, so the Prophet gave her over to him. No one won't have her very long though, for I saw death in her face yesterday. She is more like a ghost than a woman. Are you off, then?'

'Yes, I am off,' said Jefferson Hope, who had risen from his seat. His face might have been chiselled out of marble, so hard and set was its expression, while its eyes glowed with a baleful light.

'Where are you going?'

'Never mind,' he answered; and, slinging his weapon over his shoulder, strode off down the gorge and so away into the heart of the mountains to the haunts of the wild beasts. Amongst them all there was none so fierce and so dangerous as himself.

The prediction of the Mormon was only too well fulfilled. Whether it was the terrible death of her father or the effects of the hateful marriage into which she had been forced, poor Lucy never held up her head again, but pined away and died within a month. Her sottish husband, who had married her principally for the sake of John Ferrier's property, did not affect any great grief at his bereavement; but his other wives mourned over her, and sat up with her the night before the burial, as is the Mormon custom. They were grouped round the bier in the early hours of the morning, when, to their inexpressible fear and astonishment, the door was flung open, and a savage-looking, weather-beaten man in tattered garments strode into the room. Without a glance or a word to the cowering women, he walked up to the white silent figure which had once contained the pure soul of Lucy Ferrier. Stooping over her, he pressed his lips reverently to her cold forehead, and then, snatching up her hand, he took the wedding-ring from her finger. 'She shall not be buried in that,' he cried with a fierce snarl, and before an alarm could be raised sprang down the stairs and was gone. So strange and so brief was the episode that the watchers might have found it hard to believe it themselves or persuade other people of it, had it not been for the undeniable fact that the circlet of gold which marked her as having been a bride had disappeared.

For some months Jefferson Hope lingered among the mountains, leading a strange wild life, and nursing in his heart the fierce desire for vengeance which possessed him. Tales were told in the city of the weird figure which was seen prowling about the suburbs, and which haunted the lonely mountain gorges. Once a bullet whistled through Stangerson's window and flattened itself upon the wall within a foot of him. On another occasion, as Drebber passed under a cliff a great boulder crashed down on him, and he only escaped a terrible death by throwing himself upon his face. The two young Mormons were not long in discovering the reason of these attempts upon their lives and led repeated expeditions into the mountains in the hope of capturing or killing their enemy, but always without success. Then they adopted the precaution of never going out alone or after nightfall, and of having their houses guarded. After a time they were able to relax these measures, for nothing was either heard or seen of their opponent, and they hoped that time had cooled his vindictiveness.

Far from doing so, it had, if anything, augmented it. The hunter's mind was of a hard, unyielding nature, and the predominant idea of revenge had taken such complete possession of it that there was no room for any other emotion. He was, however, above all things, practical. He soon realized that even his iron constitution could not stand the incessant strain which he was putting upon it. Exposure and want of wholesome food were wearing him out. If he died like a dog among the mountains, what was to become of his revenge then? And yet such a death was sure to overtake him if he persisted. He felt that that was to play his enemy's game, so he reluctantly returned to the old Nevada mines, there to recruit his health and to amass money enough to allow him to pursue his object without privation.

His intention had been to be absent a year at the most, but a combination of unforeseen circumstances prevented his leaving the mines for nearly five. At the end of that time, however, his memory of his wrongs and his craving for revenge were quite as keen as on that memorable night when he had stood by John Ferrier's grave. Disguised, and under an assumed name, he returned to Salt Lake City, careless what became of his own life, as long as he obtained what he knew to be justice. There he found evil tidings awaiting him. There had been a schism among the Chosen People a few months before, some of the younger members of the Church having rebelled against the authority of the Elders, and the result had been the secession of a certain number of the malcontents, who had left Utah and become Gentiles. Among these had been Drebber and Stangerson; and no one knew whither they had gone. Rumour reported that Drebber had managed to convert a large part of his property into money, and that he had departed a wealthy man, while his companion, Stangerson, was comparatively poor. There was no clue at all, however, as to their whereabouts.

Many a man, however vindictive, would have abandoned all thought of revenge in the face of such a difficulty, but Jefferson Hope never faltered for a moment. With the small competence he possessed, eked out by such employment as he could pick up, he travelled from town to town through the United States in quest of his enemies. Year passed into year, his black hair turned grizzled, but still he wandered on, a human bloodhound, with his mind wholly set upon the one object to which he had devoted his life. At last his perseverance was rewarded. It was but a glance of a face in a window, but that one glance told him that Cleveland in Ohio possessed the men whom he was in pursuit of. He returned to his miserable lodgings with his plan of vengeance all arranged. It chanced, however, that Drebber, looking from his window, had recognized the vagrant in the street, and had read murder in his eyes. He hurried before a justice of the peace, accompanied by Stangerson, who had become his private secretary, and represented to him that they were in danger of their lives from the jealousy and hatred of an old rival. That evening Jefferson Hope was taken into custody, and not being able to find sureties, was detained for some weeks. When at last he was liberated it was only to find that Drebber's house was deserted, and that he and his secretary had departed for Europe.

Again the avenger had been foiled, and again his concentrated hatred urged him to continue the pursuit. Funds were wanting, however, and for some time he had to return to work, saving every dollar for his approaching journey. At last, having collected enough to keep life in him, he departed for Europe, and tracked his enemies from city to city, working his way in any menial capacity, but never overtaking the fugitives. When he reached St Petersburg, they had departed for Paris; and when he followed them there, he learned that they had just set off for Copenhagen. At the Danish capital he was again a few days late, for they had journeyed on to London, where he at last succeeded in running them to earth. As to what occurred there, we cannot do better than quote the old hunter's own account, as duly recorded in Dr Watson's Journal, to which we are already under such obligations.

6

A Continuation of the Reminiscences of John Watson MD

Our prisoner's furious resistance did not apparently indicate any ferocity in his disposition towards ourselves, for on finding himself powerless, he smiled in an affable manner, and expressed his hopes that he had not hurt any of us in the scuffle. 'I guess you're going to take me to the police-station,' he remarked to Sherlock Holmes. 'My cab's at the door. If you'll loose my legs I'll walk down to it. I'm not so light to lift as I used to be.'

Gregson and Lestrade exchanged glances, as if they thought this proposition rather a bold one; but Holmes at once took the prisoner at his word, and loosed the towel which he had bound round his ankles. He rose and stretched his legs, as though to assure himself that they were free once more. I remember that I thought to myself, as I eyed him, that I had seldom seen a more powerfully-built man; and his dark, sun-burned face bore an expression of determination and energy which was as formidable as his personal strength.

'If there's a vacant place for a chief of the police, I reckon you are the man for it,' he said, gazing with undisguised admiration at my fellow-lodger. 'The way you kept on my trail was a caution.'

'You had better come with me,' said Holmes to the two detectives.

'I can drive you,' said Lestrade.

'Good, and Gregson can come inside with me. You, too, Doctor. You have taken an interest in the case, and may as well stick to us.'

I assented gladly, and we all descended together. Our prisoner made no attempt at escape, but stepped calmly into the cab which had been his, and we followed him. Lestrade mounted the box, whipped up the horse, and brought us in a very short time to our destination. We were ushered into a small chamber, where a police inspector noted down our prisoner's name and the names of the men with whose murder he had been charged. The official was a white-faced, unemotional man, who went through his duties in a dull, mechanical way. 'The prisoner will be put before the magistrates in the course of the week,' he said; 'in the meantime, Mr Jefferson Hope, have you anything that you wish to say? I must warn you that your words will be taken down, and may be used against you.'

'I've got a good deal to say,' our prisoner said slowly. 'I want to tell you gentlemen all about it.'

'Hadn't you better reserve that for your trial?' asked the inspector.

'I may never be tried,' he answered. 'You needn't look startled. It isn't suicide I am thinking of. Are you a doctor?' He turned his fierce dark eyes upon me as he asked this last question.

'Yes, I am,' I answered.

'Then put your hand here,' he said, with a smile, motioning with his manacled wrists towards his chest.

I did so; and became at once conscious of an extraordinary throbbing and commotion which was going on inside. The walls of his chest seemed to thrill and quiver as a frail building would do inside which some powerful engine was at work. In the silence of the room I could hear a dull humming and buzzing noise which proceeded from the same source.

'Why,' I cried, 'you have an aortic aneurism!'

'That's what they call it,' he said, placidly. 'I went to a doctor last week about it, and he told me that it is bound to burst before many days passed. It has been getting worse for years. I got it from over-exposure and under-feeding[1] among the Salt Lake Mountains. I've done my work now, and I don't care how soon I go, but I should like to leave an account of the business behind me. I don't want to be remembered as a common cut-throat.'

The inspector and the two detectives had a hurried discussion as to the advisability of allowing him to tell his story.

'Do you consider, Doctor, that there is immediate danger?' the former asked.

'Most certainly there is,' I answered.

'In that case it is clearly our duty, in the interests of justice, to take his statement,' said the inspector. 'You are at liberty, sir, to give your account, which I again warn you will be taken down.'

'I'll sit down, with your leave,' the prisoner said, suiting the action to the word. 'This aneurism of mine makes me easily tired, and the tussle we had half an hour ago has not mended matters. I'm on the brink of the grave, and I am not likely to lie to you. Every word I say is the absolute truth, and how you use it is a matter of no consequence to me.'

With these words, Jefferson Hope leaned back in his chair and began the following remarkable statement. He spoke in a calm and methodical manner, as though the events which he narrated were commonplace enough. I can vouch for the accuracy of the subjoined account, for I have had access to Lestrade's notebook, in which the prisoner's words were taken down exactly as they were uttered.

'It don't much matter to you why I hated these men,' he said; 'it's enough that they were guilty of the death of two human beings – a father and a daughter – and that they had, therefore, forfeited their own lives. After the lapse of time that has passed since their crime, it was impossible for me to secure a conviction against them in any court. I knew of their guilt though, and I determined that I should be judge, jury and executioner all rolled into one. You'd have done the same, if you have any manhood in you, if you had been in my place.

'That girl that I spoke of was to have married me twenty years ago. She was forced into marrying that same Drebber, and broke her heart over it. I took the marriage ring from her dead finger, and I vowed that his last thoughts should be of the crime for which he was punished. I have carried it about with me, and have followed him and his accomplice over two continents until I caught them. They thought to tire me out, but they could not do it. If I die tomorrow, as is likely enough, I die knowing that my work in this world is done, and well done. They have perished, and by my hand. There is nothing left for me to hope for, or to desire.

'They were rich and I was poor, so that it was no easy matter for me to follow them. When I got to London my pocket was about empty, and I found that I must turn my hand to something for my living.

Driving and riding are as natural to me as walking, so I applied at a cab-owner's office, and soon got employment. I was to bring a certain sum a week to the owner, and whatever was over that I might keep for myself. There was seldom much over, but I managed to scrape along somehow. The hardest job was to learn my way about, for I reckon that of all the mazes that ever were contrived, this city is the most confusing. I had a map beside me though, and when once I had spotted the principal hotels and stations, I got on pretty well.

'It was some time before I found out where my two gentlemen were living; but I inquired and inquired until at last I dropped across them. They were at a boarding-house at Camberwell, over on the other side of the river. When once I found them out, I knew that I had them at my mercy. I had grown my beard, and there was no chance of their recognizing me. I would dog them and follow them until I saw my opportunity. I was determined that they should not escape me again.

'They were very near doing it for all that. Go where they would about London, I was always at their heels. Sometimes I followed them on my cab, and sometimes on foot, but the former was the best, for then they could not get away from me. It was only early in the morning or late at night that I could earn anything, so that I began to get behindhand with my employer. I did not mind that, however, as long as I could lay my hand upon the men I wanted.

'They were very cunning, though. They must have thought that there was some chance of their being followed, for they would never go out alone, and never after nightfall. During two weeks I drove behind them every day, and never once saw them separate. Drebber himself was drunk half the time, but Stangerson was not to be caught napping. I watched them late and early, but never saw the ghost of a chance; but I was not discouraged, for something told me that the hour had almost come. My only fear was that this thing in my chest might burst a little too soon and leave my work undone.

'At last, one evening I was driving up and down Torquay Terrace, as the street was called in which they boarded, when I saw a cab drive up to their door. Presently some luggage was brought out and after a time Drebber and Stangerson followed it, and drove off. I whipped up my horse and kept within sight of them, feeling very ill at ease, for

I feared that they were going to shift their quarters. At Euston Station they got out, and I left a boy to hold my horse and followed them on to the platform. I heard them ask for the Liverpool train, and the guard answer that one had just gone, and there would not be another for some hours. Stangerson seemed to be put out at that, but Drebber was rather pleased than otherwise. I got so close to them in the bustle that I could hear every word that passed between them. Drebber said that he had a little business of his own to do, and that if the other would wait for him he would soon rejoin him. His companion remonstrated with him, and reminded him that they had resolved to stick together. Drebber answered that the matter was a delicate one, and that he must go alone. I could not catch what Stangerson said to that, but the other burst out swearing, and reminded him that he was nothing more than his paid servant, and that he must not presume to dictate to him. On that the secretary gave it up as a bad job, and simply bargained with him that if he missed the last train he should rejoin him at Halliday's Private Hotel; to which Drebber answered that he would be back on the platform before eleven, and made his way out of the station.

'The moment for which I had waited so long had at last come. I had my enemies within my power. Together they could protect each other, but singly they were at my mercy. I did not act, however, with undue precipitation. My plans were already formed. There is no satisfaction in vengeance unless the offender has time to realize who it is that strikes him, and why retribution has come upon him. I had my plans arranged by which I should have the opportunity of making the man who had wronged me understand that his old sin had found him out. It chanced that some days before a gentleman who had been engaged in looking over some houses in the Brixton Road had dropped the key of one of them in my carriage. It was claimed that same evening, and returned; but in the interval I had taken a moulding of it, and had a duplicate constructed. By means of this I had access to at least one spot in this great city where I could rely upon being free from interruption. How to get Drebber to that house was the difficult problem which I had now to solve.

'He walked down the road and went into one or two liquor shops, staying for nearly half an hour in the last of them. When he came out, he staggered in his walk, and was evidently pretty well on. There was a hansom just in front of me, and he hailed it. I followed it so close that the nose of my horse was within a yard of his driver the whole way. We rattled across Waterloo Bridge and through miles of streets, until, to my astonishment, we found ourselves back in the terrace in which he had boarded. I could not imagine what his intention was in returning there; but I went on and pulled up my cab a hundred yards or so from the house. He entered it, and his hansom drove away. Give me a glass of water, if you please. My mouth gets dry with the talking.'

I handed him the glass, and he drank it down.

'That's better,' he said. 'Well, I waited for a quarter of an hour, or more, when suddenly there came a noise like people struggling inside the house. Next moment the door was flung open and two men appeared, one of whom was Drebber, and the other was a young man whom I had never seen before. This fellow had Drebber by the collar, and when they came to the head of the steps he gave him a shove and a kick which sent him half across the road. "You hound!" he cried, shaking his stick at him; "I'll teach you to insult an honest girl!" He was so hot that I think he would have thrashed Drebber with his cudgel, only that the cur staggered away down the road as fast as his legs would carry him. He ran as far as the corner, and then seeing my cab, he hailed me and jumped in. "Drive me to Halliday's Private Hotel," said he.

'When I had him fairly inside my cab, my heart jumped so with joy that I feared lest at this last moment my aneurism might go wrong. I drove along slowly, weighing in my own mind what it was best to do. I might take him right out into the country, and there in some deserted lane have my last interview with him. I had almost decided upon this, when he solved the problem for me. The craze for drink had seized him again, and he ordered me to pull up outside a gin palace. He went in, leaving word that I should wait for him. There he remained until closing time, and when he came out he was so far gone that I knew the game was in my own hands.

'Don't imagine that I intended to kill him in cold blood. It would only have been rigid justice if I had done so, but I could not bring myself to do it. I had long determined that he should have a show for his life if he chose to take advantage of it. Among the many billets which I have filled in America during my wandering life, I was once janitor and sweeper-out of the laboratory at York College.[2] One day the professor was lecturing on poisons, and he showed his students some alkaloid, as he called it, which he had extracted from some South American arrow poison, and which was so powerful that the least grain meant instant death. I spotted the bottle in which this preparation was kept, and when they were all gone, I helped myself to a little of it. I was a fairly good dispenser, so I worked this alkaloid into small, soluble pills, and each pill I put in a box with a similar pill made without the poison. I determined at the time that when I had my chance my gentlemen should each have a draw out of one of these boxes, while I ate the pill that remained. It would be quite as deadly and a good deal less noisy than firing across a handkerchief. From that day I had always my pill boxes about with me, and the time had now come when I was to use them.

'It was nearer one than twelve, and a wild, bleak night, blowing hard and raining in torrents. Dismal as it was outside, I was glad within – so glad that I could have shouted out from pure exultation. If any of you gentlemen have ever pined for a thing, and longed for it during twenty long years, and then suddenly found it within your reach you would understand my feelings. I lit a cigar, and puffed at it to steady my nerves, but my hands were trembling and my temples throbbing with excitement. As I drove, I could see old John Ferrier and sweet Lucy looking at me out of the darkness and smiling at me, just as plain as I see you all in this room. All the way they were ahead of me, one on each side of the horse, until I pulled up at the house in the Brixton Road.

'There was not a soul to be seen, nor a sound to be heard, except the dripping of the rain. When I looked in at the window, I found Drebber all huddled together in a drunken sleep. I shook him by the arm, "It's time to get out," I said.

' "All right, cabby," said he.

'I suppose he thought we had come to the hotel that he had mentioned, for he got out without another word, and followed me down the garden. I had to walk beside him to keep him steady, for he was still a little top-heavy. When we came to the door, I opened it, and led him into the front room. I give my word that all the way, the father and the daughter were walking in front of us.

'"It's infernally dark," said he, stamping about.

'"We'll soon have a light," I said, striking a match and putting it to a wax candle which I had brought with me. "Now, Enoch Drebber," I continued, turning to him, and holding the light to my own face, "who am I?"

'He gazed at me with bleared, drunken eyes for a moment, and then I saw a horror spring up in them, and convulse his whole features, which showed me that he knew me. He staggered back with a livid face, and I saw the perspiration break out upon his brow, while his teeth chattered in his head. At the sight I leaned my back against the door and laughed loud and long. I had always known that vengeance would be sweet, but I had never hoped for the contentment of soul which now possessed me.

'"You dog!" I said; "I have hunted you from Salt Lake City to St Petersburg, and you have always escaped me. Now, at last your wanderings have come to an end, for either you or I shall never see tomorrow's sun rise." He shrunk still farther away as I spoke, and I could see on his face that he thought I was mad. So I was for the time. The pulses in my temples beat like sledge-hammers, and I believe I would have had a fit of some sort of if the blood had not gushed from my nose and relieved me.

'"What do you think of Lucy Ferrier now?" I cried, locking the door, and shaking the key in his face. "Punishment has been slow in coming, but it has overtaken you at last." I saw his coward lips tremble as I spoke. He would have begged for his life, but he knew well that it was useless.

'"Would you murder me?" he stammered.

'"There is no murder," I answered. "Who talks of murdering a mad dog? What mercy had you upon my poor darling, when you dragged her from her slaughtered father, and bore her away to your accursed and shameless harem."

'"It was not I who killed her father," he cried.

'"But it was you who broke her innocent heart," I shrieked,

thrusting the box before him. "Let the high God judge between us. Choose and eat. There is death in one and life in the other. I shall take what you leave. Let us see if there is justice upon the earth, or if we are ruled by chance."

'He cowered away with wild cries and prayers for mercy, but I drew my knife and held it to his throat until he had obeyed me. Then I swallowed the other, and we stood facing one another in silence for a minute or more, waiting to see which was to live and which was to die. Shall I ever forget the look which came over his face when the first warning pangs told him that the poison was in his system? I laughed as I saw it, and held Lucy's marriage ring in front of his eyes. It was but for a moment, for the action of the alkaloid is rapid. A spasm of pain contorted his features; he threw his hands out in front of him, staggered, and then, with a hoarse cry, fell heavily upon the floor. I turned him over with my foot, and placed my hand upon his heart. There was no movement. He was dead!

'The blood had been streaming from my nose; but I had taken no notice of it. I don't know what it was that put it into my head to write upon the wall with it. Perhaps it was some mischievous idea of setting the police upon a wrong track, for I felt light-hearted and cheerful. I remembered a German being found in New York with RACHE written up above him, and it was argued at the time in the newspapers that the secret societies must have done it. I guessed that what puzzled the New Yorkers would puzzle the Londoners, so I dipped my finger in my own blood and printed it on a convenient place on the wall. Then I walked down to my cab and found that there was nobody about, and that the night was still very wild. I had driven some distance, when I put my hand into the pocket in which I usually kept Lucy's ring, and found that it was not there. I was thunderstruck at this, for it was the only memento that I had of her. Thinking that I might have dropped it when I stooped over Drebber's body, I drove back, and leaving my cab in a side street, I went boldly up to the house – for I was ready to dare anything rather than lose the ring. When I arrived there, I walked right into the arms of a police-officer who was coming out, and only managed to disarm his suspicions by pretending to be hopelessly drunk.

'That was how Enoch Drebber came to his end. All I had to do then was to do as much for Stangerson, and so pay off John Ferrier's debt. I knew that he was staying at Halliday's Private Hotel, and I hung about all day, but he never came out. I fancy that he suspected something when Drebber failed to put in an appearance. He was cunning, was Stangerson, and always on his guard. If he thought he could keep me off by staying indoors he was very much mistaken. I soon found out which was the window of his bedroom, and early next morning I took advantage of some ladders which were lying in the lane behind the hotel, and so made my way into his room in the grey of the dawn. I woke him up and told him that the hour had come when he was to answer for the life he had taken so long before. I described Drebber's death to him, and I gave him the same choice of the poisoned pills. Instead of grasping at the chance of safety which that offered him, he sprang from his bed and flew at my throat. In self-defence I stabbed him to the heart. It would have been the same in any case, for Providence would never have allowed his guilty hand to pick out anything but the poison.

'I have little more to say and it's as well, for I am about done up. I went on cabbing it for a day or so, intending to keep at it until I could save enough to take me back to America. I was standing in the yard when a ragged youngster asked if there was a cabby there called Jefferson Hope, and said that his cab was wanted by a gentleman at 221B, Baker Street. I went round suspecting no harm,[3] and the next thing I knew, this young man here had the bracelets on my wrists, and as neatly shackled as ever I saw in my life. That's the whole of my story, gentlemen. You may consider me to be a murderer; but I hold that I am just as much an officer of justice as you are.'

So thrilling had the man's narrative been and his manner was so impressive that we had sat silent and absorbed. Even the professional detectives, blasé as they were in every detail of crime, appeared to be keenly interested in the man's story. When he finished, we sat for some minutes in a stillness which was only broken by the scratching of Lestrade's pencil as he gave the finishing touches to his shorthand account.

'There is only one point on which I should like a little more information,' Sherlock Holmes said at last. 'Who was your accomplice who came for the ring which I advertised?'

The prisoner winked at my friend jocosely. 'I can tell my own secrets,' he said, 'but I don't get other people into trouble. I saw your advertisement, and I thought it might be a plant, or it might be the ring which I wanted. My friend volunteered to go and see. I think you'll own he did it smartly.'

'Not a doubt of that,' said Holmes heartily.

'Now, gentlemen,' the inspector remarked, gravely, 'the forms of the law must be complied with. On Thursday the prisoner will be brought before the magistrates, and your attendance will be required. Until then I will be responsible for him.' He rang the bell as he spoke, and Jefferson Hope was led off by a couple of warders, while my friend and I made our way out of the station and took a cab back to Baker Street.

7

The Conclusion

We had all been warned to appear before the magistrates upon the Thursday; but when the Thursday came there was no occasion for our testimony. A higher Judge had taken the matter in hand, and Jefferson Hope had been summoned before a tribunal where strict justice would be meted out to him. On the very night after his capture the aneurism burst, and he was found in the morning stretched upon the floor of the cell, with a placid smile upon his face, as though he had been able in his dying moments to look back upon a useful life, and on work well done.

'Gregson and Lestrade will be wild about his death,' Holmes remarked, as we chatted it over next evening. 'Where will their grand advertisement be now?'

'I don't see that they had very much to do with his capture,' I answered.

'What you do in this world is a matter of no consequence,' returned my companion, bitterly. 'The question is, what can you make people believe that you have done. Never mind,' he continued, more brightly, after a pause. 'I would not have missed the investigation for anything. There has been no better case within my recollection. Simple as it was, there were several most instructive points about it.'

'Simple!' I ejaculated.

'Well, really, it can hardly be described as otherwise,' said Sherlock Holmes, smiling at my surprise. 'The proof of its intrinsic simplicity is, that without any help save a few very ordinary deductions I was able to lay my hand upon the criminal within three days.'

'That is true,' said I.

'I have already explained to you that what is out of the common is usually a guide rather than a hindrance. In solving a problem of this sort, the grand thing is to be able to reason backwards. That is a very useful accomplishment, and a very easy one, but people do not practise it much. In the every-day affairs of life it is more useful to reason forwards, and so the other comes to be neglected. There are fifty who can reason synthetically for one who can reason analytically.'

'I confess,' said I, 'that I do not quite follow you.'

'I hardly expected that you would. Let me see if I can make it clearer. Most people, if you describe a train of events to them, will tell you what the result would be. They can put those events together in their minds, and argue from them that something will come to pass. There are few people, however, who, if you told them a result, would be able to evolve from their own inner consciousness what the steps were which led up to that result. This power is what I mean when I talk of reasoning backwards, or analytically.'

'I understand,' said I.

'Now this was a case in which you were given the result and had to find everything else for yourself. Now let me endeavour to show you the different steps in my reasoning. To begin at the beginning. I approached the house, as you know, on foot, and with my mind entirely free from all impressions. I naturally began by examining the roadway, and there, as I have already explained to you, I saw clearly the marks of a cab, which, I ascertained by inquiry, must have been there during the night. I satisfied myself that it was a cab and not a private carriage by the narrow gauge of the wheels. The ordinary London growler[1] is considerably less wide than a gentleman's brougham.[2]

'This was the first point gained. I then walked slowly down the garden path, which happened to be composed of a clay soil, peculiarly suitable for taking impressions. No doubt it appeared to you to be a mere trampled line of slush, but to my trained eyes every mark upon its surface had a meaning. There is no branch of detective science which is so important and so much neglected as the art of tracing footsteps. Happily, I have always laid great stress upon it, and much practice has made it second nature to me. I saw the heavy footmarks of the constable, but I saw also the track of the two men who had first passed through the garden. It was easy to tell that they had been before the others, because in places their marks had been entirely obliterated by the others coming upon the top of them. In this way my second link was formed, which told me that the nocturnal visitors were two in number, one remarkable for his height (as I calculated from the length of his stride) and the other fashionably dressed, to judge from the small and elegant impression left by his boots.

'On entering the house this last inference was confirmed. My well-booted man lay before me. The tall one, then, had done the murder, if murder there was. There was no wound upon the dead man's person, but the agitated expression upon his face assured me that he had foreseen his fate before it came upon him. Men who die from heart disease, or any sudden natural cause, never by any chance exhibit agitation upon their features. Having sniffed the dead man's lips, I detected a slightly sour smell, and I came to the conclusion that he had had poison forced upon him. Again, I argued that it had been forced upon him from the hatred and fear expressed upon his face. By the method of exclusion, I had arrived at this result, for no other hypothesis would meet the facts. Do not imagine that it was a very unheard-of idea. The forcible administration of poison is by no means a new thing in criminal annals. The cases of Dolsky in Odessa, and of Leturier in Montpellier, will occur at once to any toxicologist.

'And now came the great question as to the reason why. Robbery had not been the object of the murder, for nothing was taken. Was it politics, then, or was it a woman? That was the question which confronted me. I was inclined from the first to the latter supposition. Political assassins are only too glad to do their work and to fly. This murder had, on the contrary, been done most deliberately, and the perpetrator had left his tracks all over the room, showing that he had been there all the time. It must have been a private wrong, and not a political one, which called for such a methodical revenge. When the inscription was discovered upon the wall, I was more inclined than ever to my opinion. The thing was too evidently a blind. When the ring was found, however, it settled the question. Clearly the murderer had used it to remind his victim of some dead or absent woman. It was at this point that I asked Gregson whether he had inquired in his telegram to Cleveland as to any particular point in Mr Drebber's former career. He answered, you remember, in the negative.

'I then proceeded to make a careful examination of the room, which confirmed me in my opinion as to the murderer's height, and furnished me with the additional details as to the Trichinopoly cigar and the length of his nails. I had already come to the conclusion, since there were no signs of a struggle, that the blood which covered the floor had burst from the murderer's nose in his excitement. I could perceive that the track of blood coincided with the track of his feet. It is seldom that any man, unless he is very full-blooded, breaks out in this way through emotion, so I hazarded the opinion that the criminal was probably a robust and ruddy-faced man. Events proved that I had judged correctly.

'Having left the house, I proceeded to do what Gregson had neglected. I telegraphed to the head of the police at Cleveland, limiting my inquiry to the circumstances connected with the marriage of Enoch Drebber. The answer was conclusive. It told me that Drebber had already applied for the protection of the law against an old rival in love, named Jefferson Hope, and that this same Hope was at present in Europe. I knew now that I held the clue to the mystery in my hand, and all that remained was to secure the murderer.

'I had already determined in my own mind that the man who had walked into the house with Drebber was none other than the man who had driven the cab. The marks in the road showed me that the horse had wandered on in a way which would have been impossible had there been anyone in charge of it. Where, then, could the driver be, unless he were inside the house? Again, it is absurd to suppose that any sane man would carry out a deliberate crime under the very eyes, as it were, of a third person, who was sure to betray him. Lastly, supposing one man wished to dog another through London, what better means could he adopt than to turn cabdriver. All these considerations led me to the irresistible conclusion that Jefferson Hope was to be found among the jarveys[3] of the Metropolis.

'If he had been one, there was no reason to believe that he had ceased to be. On the contrary from his point of view, any sudden change would be likely to draw attention to himself. He would probably, for a time at least, continue to perform his duties. There was no reason to suppose that he was going under an assumed name. Why should he change his name in a country where no one knew his original one? I therefore organized my Street Arab detective corps, and sent them systematically to every cab proprietor in London until they ferreted out the man that I wanted. How well they succeeded, and how quickly I took advantage of it, are still fresh in your recollection. The murder of Stangerson was an incident which was entirely unexpected, but which could hardly in any case have been prevented. Through it, as you know, I came into possession of the pills, the existence of which I had already surmised. You see, the whole thing is a chain of logical sequences without a break or flaw.'

'It is wonderful!' I cried. 'Your merits should be publicly recognized. You should publish an account of the case. If you won't, I will for you.'

'You may do what you like, Doctor,' he answered. 'See here!' he continued, handing a paper over to me, 'look at this!'

It was the *Echo* for the day, and the paragraph to which he pointed was devoted to the case in question.

'The public,' it said, 'have lost a sensational treat through the sudden death of the man Hope, who was suspected of the murder of Mr Enoch Drebber and of Mr Joseph Stangerson. The details of the case will probably be never known now, though we are informed upon good authority that the crime was the result of an old-standing and romantic feud, in which love and Mormonism bore a part. It seems that both the victims belonged, in their younger days, to the Latter Day Saints, and Hope, the deceased prisoner, hails also from Salt Lake City. If the case has had no other effect, it, at least, brings out in the most striking manner the efficiency of our detective police force, and will serve as a lesson to all foreigners that they will do wisely to settle their feuds at home, and not to carry them on to British soil. It is an open secret that the credit of this smart capture belongs entirely to the well-known Scotland Yard officials, Messrs Lestrade and Gregson. The man was apprehended, it appears, in the rooms of a certain Mr Sherlock Holmes, who has himself, as an amateur, shown some talent in the detective line, and who, with such instructors may hope in time to attain to some degree of their skill. It is expected that a testimonial of some sort will be presented to the two officers as a fitting recognition of their services.'

'Didn't I tell you so when we started?' cried Sherlock Holmes, with a laugh. 'That's the result of all our Study in Scarlet; to get them a testimonial!'

'Never mind,' I answered; 'I have all the facts in my journal, and the public shall know them. In the meantime you must make yourself contented by the consciousness of success, like the Roman miser:

' "Populus me sibilat, at mihi plaudo
Ipse domi simul ac nummos contemplar in arca." '[4]

NOTES

First published in Beeton's Christmas Annual 1887. Originally planned title *A Tangled Skein*. Most Holmes commentators believe the story to be set in 1881 in Holmesian time.

PART ONE

Being a reprint from the reminiscences of John H. Watson MD, late of the Army Medical Department

CHAPTER I
Mr Sherlock Holmes

1. *I took my degree of Doctor of Medicine*: Conan Doyle received his degree in medicine at Edinburgh University in 1885.

2. *University of London*: The university was created in 1836 as an umbrella body to administer exams for students of the Anglican King's College and the non-Anglican University College. In 1878 (Watson's day) it was based in Burlington Gardens, Mayfair, in the building that later housed the Museum of Mankind.

3. *Netley*: The Royal Victoria Military Hospital at Netley, near Southampton, built in 1856 after the Crimean War.

4. *Fusiliers*: Soldiers armed with a fusil, or flintlock musket.

5. *the second Afghan war*: The second Afghan War (1878–80) began out of Britain's concern with Russian designs on the mountainous country and, it was feared, on India, over which Queen Victoria had been declared Empress in 1876. On 21 November 1878 the British Army entered Afghanistan through its three passes and met resistance, but soon took Jalalabad and Candahar (also known as Kandahar and Qandahar). By October 1879 Britain had gained control of Kabul, the capital, and Afghan leaders gave Britain control of foreign policy and ownership of large portions of land. Afghanistan gained its independence in 1919 following the third Afghan War.

6. *Candahar*: At the beginning of the second Afghan War, Sir Donald Stewart entered Candahar via the Bolan Pass and used it as his headquarters before marching on Kabul late in 1879 to quash a tribal uprising against the occupying British force. Ayub Khan advanced on Candahar and beseiged it during his 1880 uprising against British peace terms, but General Sir Frederick Roberts marched 10,000 men 313 miles in twenty-two days to beat off Khan's forces. When later ennobled the victorious Roberts took the title Lord Roberts of Candahar.

7. *honours and promotion to many*: For instance Sir Donald Stewart who led the march on Kabul (see n. 6) was made KCB in 1879 and Commander-in-Chief of India 1880–85.

8. *Berkshires*: The Royal Berkshire Regiment, founded in the West Indies in 1714.

9. *Battle of Maiwand*: On 27 July 1880, Ayub Khan, opposed to British peace terms in Afghanistan, marched on Maiwand. The British and Afghan armies clashed for three hours during the middle of the day and the Afghans eventually gained the upper hand. Maiwand was one of the home country's few victorious battles during the war.

10. *Jezail bullet*: A bullet from an Afghan gun consisting of bits of rusty metal and nails.

11. *subclavian artery*: Artery at the base of the neck.

12. *Ghazis*: Fierce Muslim warriors geared towards eliminating infidels. The word comes from the Arabic verb to fight.

13. *threw me across a pack-horse, and succeeded in bringing me safely to the British lines*: As Owen Dudley Edwards has pointed out, this is reminiscent of the story of Dr William Bryden, a casualty of the first Afghan War (1839–42), who rode wounded and separated from his colleagues into Jalalabad.

14. *Peshawar*: City in Pakistan, eleven miles from the Khyber Pass, renowned for its bread stuffed with fruit.

15. *Orontes*: The ship, named after the Lebanese river, brought back injured soldiers from the Afghan campaign and called in at Portsmouth where Conan Doyle lived and practised medicine in the 1880s. Occasionally Conan Doyle's surgery received passengers from the ship.

16. *as free as an income of eleven shillings and sixpence a day will permit a man to be*:

Watson is relatively poor for an Army doctor but several stages away from incarceration in the workhouse.

17. *Criterion Bar*: The Criterion Restaurant at 224 Piccadilly was built in 1873 on the site of the White Bear Inn, which had been one of the busiest coaching inns in central London. By the 1880s it was attracting racing men and ex-soldiers in the Watson mould. In *The 'Varsity Students' Rag* (1932), John Betjeman cited the Criterion's Grill Room as the kind of place where high-spirited students were likely to make merry. A plaque commemorating the meeting of Watson and Stamford that hung in the Criterion was stolen in the 1960s and has never been found.

18. *Bart's*: St Bartholomew's, London's oldest hospital, located on Giltspur Street, Smithfield. It was founded in 1123 by Rahere, jester to Henry I, who was taken ill on a pilgrimage and vowed to found a hospital dedicated to St Bartholomew if he survived.

19. *the Holborn*: Ornate, classically designed Victorian restaurant, demolished in 1935, that stood at 218 High Holborn and had previously been the Holborn Casino, which had become the largest dance hall in London by the 1870s. Given that Watson has already revealed the need to alter his style of living, he has chosen an expensive establishment in which to have lunch.

20. *hansom*: A one-horse two-wheeled carriage named after Joseph Aloysius Hansom (1803–82) and one of the fastest means of getting across London at that time.

21. *vegetable alkaloid*: The first vegetable alkaloid to be unearthed was impure nicotine in 1803. Other similar substances include strychnine, caffeine and quinine.

22. *beating the subjects in the dissecting-rooms with a stick*: Similar tests were done to test how the bruises may have formed on a corpse found in the possession of William Burke (1792–1829), the infamous bodysnatcher. Corpses of animals and human beings were struck at intervals and eventually the authorities decided that Burke's claim, that the bruises resulted from rough handling in packing the deceased, could be true.

23. *Bunsen lamps*: Named after German chemist Robert Wilhelm Eberhard Bunsen (1811–99). The tube is approximately six inches long and has an extension at the base to allow the entry of the gas mixture that is burnt at the top end.

24. *You have been in Afghanistan, I perceive*: Perhaps the most famous introductory line in literature, and based on the banter between Dr Johnson and Boswell regarding the latter's coming from Scotland when they first met in Thomas Davies's Covent Garden bookshop in 1763.

25. *The old guaiacum test*: Named after the guaiacum tree of the West Indies and South America. The test involves preparing a tincture of one part resin to six parts alcohol, which is then added to a smaller quantity of the liquid being tested and shaken with a few drops of hydrogen peroxide in ether. The ether dissolves the resin and, if blood is present, the mixture turns bright blue. **26**. *the Sherlock Holmes test*: Holmes never refers to the test again anywhere in the canon.

27. *the notorious Muller*: Possibly inspired by Franz Müller, who in 1864 became the first railway murderer and was convicted after absentmindedly going off with his victim's hat.

28. *I keep a bull pup*: Evidently it got lost somewhere between Watson's Strand hotel and his new lodgings in Baker Street for it is never referred to again. Owen Dudley Edwards offers the alternative explanation that Watson is using bull pup for bulldog, a short-barrelled revolver.

29. *The proper study of mankind is man*:

Know then thyself, presume not God to scan;

The proper study of mankind is man.

Alexander Pope, *An Essay on Man*, Epistle II, 1–2

CHAPTER 2
The Science of Deduction

1. *No. 221B Baker Street*: More words have been written trying to find the location of what is probably the most famous address in literature than on any other topic in the Holmes canon. Conan Doyle himself gave no clues about the identity of 221B apart from the 'B' (short for *bis*, from the Italian for having some more) which implies that the rooms are supposed to be above a shop, and Baker Street itself was then about half its current length (the northern boundary being Crawford Street/Paddington Street), with the numbers only reaching as high as 85. In his original notes Conan Doyle had J. Sherrinford Holmes and Ormond Sacker (the nominal prototypes for Holmes and Watson) living at 221B *Upper* Baker Street, which was the name of what is now the short section of Baker Street north of Marylebone Road. Its numbers failed to reach three figures, let alone 221B.

Holmes scholars have suggested various Baker Street houses as the original model: No. 21, because Conan Doyle had supposedly erroneously written the address with a superfluous '2' when working on *A Study In Scarlet*; the recently demolished No. 31 (then No. 72), because the property had a back yard large enough to accommodate a 'solitary plane tree' (as revealed in 'The Problem Of Thor Bridge' from *The Casebook of Sherlock Holmes*); and either of two properties opposite the real-life Camden House (the 'Empty House' in the story of the same name). In 1894, these were 30 York Place (now 111 Baker Street), home of the Portman Estate Office (and now a post office), or 29 York Place (now 109 Baker Street), a boys' school (now offices for several companies).

In 1930 the council extended Baker Street north, which then made a Georgian house that had been 41 Upper Baker Street at the time of *A Study In Scarlet*'s publication No. 221 Baker Street. Soon after, the house was demolished and replaced by Abbey House (Nos 215–29), headquarters of the Abbey National Bank and Building Society. During the 1951 Festival of Britain, Abbey House staged an exhibition of Sherlock Holmes with a reconstruction of the 221B sitting-room (now situated in the Sherlock Holmes pub near the Strand) and the office still receives around forty letters a month addressed to Holmes and Watson. In the 1990s a restaurant opened at No. 239 a few yards north disingenuously sporting the 221B address.

2. *lowest portions of the city*: To Victorian novelists the impoverished, disease-ridden slums were an endless source of fascination; even today dark corners of London such as Bankside, Borough, Vauxhall or Wapping are described as 'Dickensian'. Conan Doyle may have contemplated Holmes's exploring 'the lowest portions of the city' (which in 1887 would have included the above districts and many more in the centre – Seven Dials, St Giles, Farringdon, for instance – that have long since been cleaned up) but included insufficient descriptions of Holmes in such quarters to merit the adjective 'Doylian', or even Holmesian, for describing such parts of London.

3. *His very person and appearance*: In his autobiography, *Memories and Adventures*, Conan Doyle explained that Holmes 'had . . . a thin razor-like face, with a great hawk's-bill of a nose, and two small eyes, set close together on one side of it.' Early pictures of Holmes were drawn by Sidney Paget, who based them on his brother, Walter.

4. *Upon my quoting Thomas Carlyle, he inquired in the naïvest way who he might be and what he had done*: Although this comes across as a pithy and memorable put-down of the Scottish historian and essayist (1795–1881), Conan Doyle's target was more likely to have been ignorant, uncultured medical students. Ironically, a few chapters later Holmes quotes a famous Carlyle epigram: 'Genius is an infinite capacity for taking pains.'

5. *ignorant of the Copernican Theory and of the composition of the Solar System*: In *De revolutionibus orbium coelestium*: Polish astronomer Nicholas Copernicus (1473–1543) became the first person to successfully propose the idea that the sun was at the centre of the solar system and that the earth and other planets revolved around it. Until then it was assumed that the earth stood still and the sun moved around it (as one might surmise from Joshua 10:12–13, in which the Hebrew leader successfully commands the sun to stand still).

6. *A fool takes in all the lumber of every sort that he comes across*: Nearly forty years later, in 'The Lion's Mane' from *The Casebook Of Sherlock Holmes* (1927), the detective admits that his mind is a boxroom crowded with unsystematic and out-of-the-way knowledge.

7. *useless facts elbowing out the useful ones*: Later in the canon, in *The Valley Of Fear* (1915), Holmes changes his mind, extolling the 'oblique uses of knowledge'.

8. *Knowledge of Literature: Nil*: In later stories Holmes quotes from the Bible, Horace, Tacitus, Shakespeare, Thoreau, Flaubert (incorrectly) and Goethe, and compares Horace with Hafiz.

9. *Knowledge of Philosophy: Nil*: By the time we reach *His Last Bow* Holmes, as Watson notes in 'his' preface, is in retirement and dividing his time between philosophy and agriculture.

10. *Knowledge of Astronomy: Nil*: In 'The Greek Interpreter' from *The Memoirs of Sherlock Holmes* (1893), Holmes's knowledge of astronomy is profound enough to be able to speculate on changes in the obliquity of the ecliptic.

11. *Knowledge of Politics: Feeble*: In 'A Scandal in Bohemia' from *The Adventures of Sherlock Holmes* (1892), Holmes, on realizing that his masked visitor is the King of Bohemia, quickly announces, 'Your Majesty had not spoken before I was aware that I was addressing Wilhelm Gottsreich Sigismond von Ormstein, Grand Duke of Cassel-Falstein, and hereditary King of Bohemia.'

12. *singlestick*: A wooden stick used instead of a sword in fencing. Singlesticks are nearly three feet long, made of hickory or oak, and have a guard to protect the player's hand.

13. *Mendelssohn's Lieder*: The *Lieder ohne Wortes* (Songs Without Words) of Jakob Ludwig Felix Mendelssohn-Bartholdy (1809–47).

14. *one little sallow, rat-faced, dark-eyed fellow who was introduced to me as Mr Lestrade*: By the time of *The Hound of the Baskervilles* (1902) Lestrade, despite minimum height requirements needed to get into the force, has metamorphosed into a 'small, wiry bulldog of a man'. Lestrade's tenure in the Holmes canon is so long that Gavin Brend was inspired to write the following epigram:

> A life of ease I am much afraid
> Was denied to Inspector G. Lestrade
> With the *Study in Scarlet* in '81
> You'd think that his job had just begun.
> But nevertheless the fact appears
> He'd already put in some twenty years.
> And yet if the Garrideb case be true
> He was still at the Yard in 1902.
> I feel it must be exceedingly hard
> To spend forty years at Scotland Yard.

15. *The Book of Life*: The title is taken from *Revelation* 20:12: 'And I saw the dead, small and great, stand before God; and the books were opened: and another book was opened, which is the book of life . . .'

16. *Euclid*: Greek mathematician of the fourth century BC who proposed a series of theorems and problems which form the basis of geometry.

17. *Where in the tropics*: Afghanistan is not in the tropics. Watson could have received such injuries – and a better tan – in South Africa where the British army waged war against the Zulus 1879–80.

18. *Dupin*: Amateur detective and hero of Poe's 'The Murders in the Rue Morgue' (1841), 'The Purloined Letter' (1845), and 'The Mystery of Marie Roget' (1842)

19. *Dupin was a very inferior fellow*: Conan Doyle has twisted his view of Dupin for dramatic effect. In real life he regularly acknowledged his debt to Poe whom he considered to be the 'supreme original short story writer' and whose stories he would place second to Macaulay's essays.

20. *Gaboriau's works*: The works of the French novelist Emile Gaboriau (1833–73) who wrote five stories about the detective M. Lecoq.

21. *Scotland Yard*: Headquarters of the Metropolitan Police, then at 4 Whitehall Place, Westminster, on the site of the palace where visiting Scottish kings had stayed when visiting London.

22. *Commissionaire*: One of the Corps of Commissionaires, uniformed messengers consisting of retired soldiers and sailors founded in 1859 by Captain Sir Edward Walter.

23. *Royal Marine Light Infantry*: Branch of the army involved in marine combat.

CHAPTER 3
The Lauriston Gardens Mystery

1. *Would you mind reading it to me aloud?*: Holmes often asks Watson to read out correspondence to him, but it is not made clear whether or not he is suffering from hypermetropia (ability to see clearly from afar but not at close range) and thus be able to analyse a tattoo on the hand of a man standing in the street from the window of 221B Baker street yet not be able to read a letter at close distance.

2. *Lauriston Gardens*: Based on Nos 152–60 Brixton Road, a row of houses built in 1828 and now known as Herbert Morrison Terrace after the post-war Labour politician.

3. *Cremona fiddles, and the difference between a Stradivarius and an Amati*: The Amati of Cremona were a family of sixteenth- and seventeenth- century violin makers whose most famous pupil was Antonio Stradivari (1644–1737), maker of at least a thousand violins between 1666 and 1737.

4. *You did not come here in a cab?*: What seems to be a throwaway line is in fact the first query relating to a criminal investigation (as revealed later in the story) uttered by Holmes in the entire canon.

5. *There is nothing new under the sun*: Adapted from 'There is no new thing under the sun', Ecclesiastes 1:9.

6. *Barraud*: Firm then based at 41 Cornhill in the City of London.

7. *Gold Albert chain*: A watch chain made of heavy links named after Prince Albert (1819–61), husband of Queen Victoria.

8. *Boccaccio's* Decameron: Between 1348 and 1353 Giovanni Boccaccio (1313–75) wrote the *Decameron*, a collection of tales in which ten young people fleeing plague-stricken Florence amuse each other by telling a story on the days they spend together.

9. *American Exchange, Strand*: A kiosk that stood outside Charing Cross station, which London-based Americans could use as a postal address and where a wide range of US newspapers could be bought. In 'The Illustrious Client' from *The Casebook Of Sherlock Holmes* (1927), Watson catches a glimpse of the shocking headline – 'Murderous Attack on Sherlock Holmes' – on the newspaper being displayed by the one-legged news-vendor positioned at the same spot.

10. *Guion Steamship Company*: The company's *Atlantic* was the first ship to cross the Atlantic in under a week.

11. *They say that genius is an infinite capacity for taking pains*: Epigram by Thomas Carlyle from *Frederick the Great*, Book IV, Chapter 3. Earlier in the story Holmes had expressed ignorance of who Carlyle was.

12. *Kennington Park Gate*: Kennington Park stands at the junction of Kennington Park Road and Camberwell Road. There is no Kennington Park Gate.

13. *There has been murder done*: Rarer in the Holmes canon than one would think. The detective investigates only eight murders in the entire canon.

14. *in the prime of life*: This turns out to be one of the few points on which Holmes is wrong, but is a minor part of his analysis.

15. *Trichinopoly cigar*: A pierced cigar open at both ends made of tobacco grown near Trichinopoly, a city in the Madras district of India. It was often sold with a straw inserted through the opening to keep it clear until it was smoked.

16. *Parthian shot*: Hostile remark made while leaving. The ancient cavalry of Parthia used to shoot backwards (unexpectedly) as they departed.

CHAPTER 4
What John Rance Had To Tell

1. *sere and yellow*: 'I have lived long enough. My way of life/Is fall'n into the sere, the yellow leaf.' Macbeth from Shakespeare's *Macbeth* V, iii, 22–3.

2. *Socialism and secret societies*: In the 1880s socialism was not quite comparable to today's definition of socialism as an ideology compatible with parliamentary democracy, geared towards central planning and sympathetic to trade unionists and other social groups, but was a cause espoused by quasi-revolutionary extra-parliamentary groups. Conan Doyle, writing *A Study in Scarlet* in 1887, would have easily recalled many stories of socialist atrocities – armed robberies, dynamitings – recently committed in London, usually by foreign revolutionaries. As Michael Harrison outlined in *In The Footsteps Of Sherlock Holmes* (David & Charles, Newton Abbot, 1958), on 16 March 1881 there was an attempt to blow up Mansion House in the City of London. Two years later on the same day a bomb exploded near the Local Government Office on Charles Street, Whitehall. Bombers also targeted the London Underground on 30 October 1883, placing a nitro-glycerine charge in the tunnel between Charing Cross and Westminster stations. On the same day at 8. 13 p.m. a bomb went off in a third-class carriage near Paddington station, injuring 62 people. On 30 May 1884 two bombs went off on the same day at the same time, one at Scotland Yard police headquarters and one at the Junior Carlton club half a mile west. Also, sixteen cakes of dynamite were found at the base of Nelson's Column that day but were defused. The outrages stopped soon after one of their number, a Rolla Richards, was imprisoned in 1897, although a few weeks after his conviction a bomb at Aldersgate (now Barbican) station killed one man.

3. *after the German fashion*: German was printed in Gothic script.

4. *in the Latin character*: As used in English books.

5. *Hallé's concert*: A concert with Karl (later Charles) Hallé (1819–95), German musician and conductor, who came to England in 1843 and later to Manchester where, in 1858, he founded the Hallé Orchestra, one of the few orchestras in Britain named after an individual rather than the place of origination. Hallé staged an annual series in London from 1861 and introduced the works of Hector Berlioz and Frederic Chopin to Britain.

6. *Norman-Neruda*: Wilma Norman-Neruda (1839–1911), a Moravian violinist who, after the death of her first husband, Ludwig Norman, married Charles Hallé, and later became violinist to Queen Victoria.

7. *Holmes took a half-sovereign from his pocket*: In 1878, three in four chief inspectors of what was then the Detective Branch of the Metropolitan Police (what *Punch* later referred to as the Defective Department and what is now the Criminal Investigations Department or CID) were found guilty of corruption.

8. *White Hart*: The White Hart pub stood at the junction of Loughborough Road and Lilford Road, Brixton, and has now been converted to flats although the relief of the animal can be seen in the stone work.

9. *Holland Grove*: A street in north Brixton to the south-east of the Oval cricket ground.

10. *Henrietta Street*: Fictitious.

11. *Brixton Road*: The main road through the area running north to south for two miles from Kennington Park to the junction of Acre Lane and Cold-harbour Lane.

12. *a four of gin hot*: Fourpence worth of gin with hot water and lemon.

13. *Columbine's New-fangled Banner*: Interestingly, the drunk is singing American songs ('Hail, Columbia!' and 'The Star-Spangled Banner') not, as one would expect, English or Irish songs.

14. *scarlet thread*: 'Thy lips are like a thread of scarlet''. *Song of Solomon* 4:3.

15. *Her attack and her bowing are splendid. What's that little thing of Chopin's she plays so magnificently*: Conan Doyle is revealing his well-known ignorance of music; Chopin never wrote any music for solo violin and Mme Norman-Neruda played no Chopin pieces arranged for the violin in 1887 (when *A Study In Scarlet* was published).

CHAPTER 5
Our Advertisement Brings a Visitor

1. *If ever human features bespoke vice of the most malignant type*: Cesare Lombroso's *L'uomo delinquente* (1875) propounded the idea that there could be such a thing as a criminal human type, and detective novels and films, particularly comedies, have had much service out of the notion over the last hundred years. The theory was hilariously sent up by Kenneth Williams playing the part of the naïve Sgt Benson in Gerald Thomas's 1960 film *Carry on Constable*.

2. *what Darwin says about music*: In *The Descent of Man* (1885, p. 572), Charles Darwin (1809–82) wrote: 'As we have every reason to suppose that articulate speech is one of the latest, as it is certainly the highest, of the arts acquired by man, and as the instinctive power of producing musical notes and rhythm is developed low down in the animal series, it would be altogether opposed to the principle of evolution, if we were to admit that man's musical capacity has been developed from the tones used in impassioned speech.'

3. *My old service revolver*: This would have been either an Adams 6-shot .450

cal. breech-loader which was standard in the British Army during the second Afghan War, or a .442/.450 Solid Frame Webley Double Action.

4. *De Jure inter Gentes*: 'Of the Law between Peoples', from either *De Jure Naturae et Getium* by Samuel Profendorf, published in 1672, or the same title by Richard Zouche (1590–1661), published in 1651.

5. *Charles's head was still firm on his shoulders*: Charles being Charles I, King of England, from 1625 until he was beheaded in 1649.

6. *Philippe de Croy, whoever he may have been*: Flemish nobleman Philippe de Croy (1526–95), third Duke of Aerschot.

7. *William Whyte*: William White (1604–78) wrote several Latin works as Gulielmus Phalerius.

8. *a Union boat*: A Union Line steamer that plied the route to South Africa.

9. *13, Duncan Street, Houndsditch*: Duncan Street is taken from an Edinburgh thoroughfare known to Conan Doyle. Houndsditch is an important street in the City of London named after a ditch in which people would often leave their dead dogs.

10. *Mayfield Place, Peckham*: Mayfield Place is again an Edinburgh turning. Peckham is a suburb of faded glory in south-east London which was semi-respectable in Victorian times.

11. *ulster*: Ulster overcoat introduced by the firm of John G. McGee & Co of Belfast, Ulster, in 1867.

12. *cravat*: The word also has Irish origins, a *carabhat* being a neck-cloth in Gaelic. The practice of wearing such attire by the peoples of the eastern Adriatic Coast led to the area being known as Hrvatska, which has been anglicized as Croatia.

13. *Henri Murger's* Vie de Bohème: *Scènes de la vie de Bohème*, an 1848 collection of stories by Henri Murger (1822–61), a former secretary to Count Aleksei Tolstoi, describes the fortunes of a group of students and artists in Paris. Puccini's opera *La Bohème* (1898) was based on it.

CHAPTER 6
Tobias Gregson Shows What He Can Do

1. *Vehmgericht*: Secret courts in medieval Germany set up to exact revenge and run by a society which all freemen were eligible to join. They were abolished in 1811.

2. *aqua tofana*: Poison named after a Sicilian woman, Tofana.

3. *Carbonari*: Secret society of early nineteenth-century Italian patriots whose members met in the forests and posed as woodcutters or charcoal-burners (*carbonari* is the Italian for charcoal burners).

4. *Marchioness de Brinvilliers*: Marie Madeleine d'Aubray (*c.*1630–76), a French woman who poisoned her father, brother and sisters.

5. *the Darwinian theory*: The theory of evolution through natural selection as postulated by the English scientist Charles Darwin (1809–82)

6. *the principles of Malthus*: Thomas Robert Malthus (1766–1834), English clergyman and political economist, claimed in his *Essay on Population* (1798) that the population would increase geometrically while resources increased only arithmetically and therefore the world's population would go hungry before long. Evidence over the last two hundred years suggests that Malthus was wrong.

7. *the Ratcliff Highway murders*: On 7 December 1811 an unknown assailant struck at 29 Ratcliff Highway, Wapping, a house in a rough part of the east London docks area, and murdered draper Timothy Marr, Marr's wife, their baby and a boy apprentice. The victims were discovered when the maid returned from buying oysters and found her knocks unanswered. A few days later Williamson, the publican of the King's Arms pub at 81 New Gravel Lane, Shadwell, half a mile away, his wife, and their maid, were found with their throats cut. John Williams, a seaman who had been shipmates with Marr, was arrested and charged with the murders. The evidence against him was circumstantial but he hanged himself before he could be tried.

Thomas De Quincey wrote a satirical essay about the events, 'Murder Considered as One of the Fine Arts' (1827), in which he described how Williams 'asserted his own supremacy above all the children of Cain', claiming that the Ratcliff Highway murders were 'the most superb of the century by many degrees'. The crimes still captivate modern-day writers including Peter Ackroyd, Iain Sinclair, and P. D. James who co-wrote a book about the case, *The Maul and The Pear Tree*, so named because a maul was found at the site of the first murders and Williams had been lodging at the Pear Tree pub, half a mile east of 29 Ratcliff Highway, when arrested. All the relevant addresses have since been demolished.

8. *Liberal Administration*: William Ewart Gladstone (1809–98) became prime minister for the second time in April 1880 (*A Study in Scarlet* is supposed to be set in 1881). At this time Conan Doyle was a Gladstone supporter.

9. *Torquay Terrace, Camberwell*: Fictitious address in the south-east London inner suburb.

10. *the 4th inst.,*: The 4th instant, a Latinized way of saying the 4th of the present month.

11. *Euston Station*: London's oldest railway terminus serving the West Midlands, the north-west of England and west Scotland.

12. Un sot trouve toujours un plus sot qui l'admire: 'A fool can always find a greater fool to admire him', from Line 232 of Canto I of *L'Art Poétique* by Nicolas Boileau Despréaux (1636–1711).

PART TWO

The Country of the Saints

CHAPTER I
On the Great Alkali Plain

1. *Pawnees*: An Indian tribe that inhabited the region between the Missouri River and the Rockies. Their numbers decreased from 10,000 to around 4,500 after a cholera epidemic in 1846. Two thousand-odd survivors now live in Pawnee, Oklahoma.

2. *Blackfeet*: Indian tribe living in the valleys of the Saskatchewan river. By 1850 they had moved south into the Rockies to occupy a huge area. They now live on the Blackfoot Reservation in Montana.

3. *Sierra Blanco*: Strictly the Sierra Blanca, a mountain range in New Mexico 600 miles south of the Mormon trail.

4. *eighteen hundred and forty-seven*: Chosen by Conan Doyle, presumably, as this was the year of the Irish famine.

5. *Mr Bender*: The Benders were not a family of, but individual, mystical cannibals who operated in this area.

6. *Missouri*: The second-longest river in the USA and the name of a state alongside the river.

7. *Rio Grande*: A river that rises in the Rocky Mountains and flows into the Gulf of Mexico, forming the border between Texas and Mexico along the way.

8. *Nigh upon ten thousand*: Brigham Young (see n. 14, below), in his own account of the 1847 journey to the Great Salt Lake Valley, claimed that he was accompanied by 143 men, three women and two children.

9. *the Angel Merona*: This should be Moroni, i.e. the Angel Moroni, the son of Mormon, who supposedly appeared in a vision before Joseph Smith in Palmyra, New York, in 1823. 'The Book of Moroni' is the last book in *The Book of Mormon*, which is supposed to be the word of an ancient American prophet revealed to and translated by Joseph Smith.

10. *holy Joseph Smith at Palmyra*: In 1820, when he was fourteen, Joseph Smith (1805–44) went into the woods near his home in New York State to ask the Lord in prayer 'which of all the sects was right'. In answer to his prayers 'two personages, whose brightness and glory defy all description' appeared to him.

Three years later, on 21 September 1823, Smith claimed that the angel Moroni appeared to him in Palmyra, New York, to reveal the existence of ancient texts inscribed on gold plates (*The Book of Mormon*) containing the history of a people descended from an Israelite tribe who had settled in America for the thousand years between 600 BC and AD 420.

11. *Nauvoo*: What had been the small settlement of Commerce, Illinois, on the east bank of the Mississippi in Hancock County, was transformed in 1839 into the Mormon City of Nauvoo, Illinois. Within a year it had a population of 20,000, its own militia, and began taking converts from Britain following a visit by Brigham Young. The Nauvoo Mormons soon found they held the balance of power between the local Whigs and Democrats and Smith announced himself as a candidate for the US presidency in the 1844 elections. But his campaign was thwarted by the rise of a dissident faction opposed to the prevalent Mormon practice of polygamy which published a hostile article in a newspaper, *The Nauvoo Expositor*. On Smith's orders the press was destroyed and copies of the paper burnt. Smith was jailed, a riot ensued and Smith and his brother, Hyrum, were murdered when a mob stormed their jail in Carthage, Illinois. The Mormons then abandoned Nauvoo.

12. . . . *you are the Mormons* . . . *We are the Mormons*: In 1827 Smith translated the ancient texts that had appeared to him and named them *The Book of Mormon*, after one of the later prophets who had settled in America for the thousand years between 600 BC and AD 420, i.e. one of the latter-day saints. *The Book of Mormon* was first published in Palmyra in 1830, the year in which Smith founded the Church of Jesus Christ of the Latter Day Saints, in Fayette, New York. George Orwell evidently enjoyed the conversation between Ferrier and the wandering tribe, adapting it for the moment in *1984* when Winston Smith and Julia's tryst is broken up by the secret police: "We are the dead," echoed Julia dutifully. "You are the dead," said an iron voice behind them.'

13. *On, on to Zion*: In 1831 a colony had settled in Jackson County, Missouri, later dedicated as the City of Zion.

14. *Brigham Young*: Young took over as Mormonism's major figure following Smith's murder and led the great migration west in 1846–7 that eventually reached what is now Salt Lake City. During his 30-year stewardship the Mormons settled and developed the Utah area.

CHAPTER 2
The Flower of Utah

1. *Salt Lake City*: Young arrived here for the first time on 24 July 1847, claiming he had seen it in a vision. That August he named it the City of the Great Salt

Lake. City blocks of 10 acres were divided into 1¼-acre lots for businessmen while bigger portions were handed to mechanics and farmers.

2. *great inland sea*: The Great Salt Lake.

3. *Latter Day Saints*: The Mormons' name for themselves.

4. *gold fever*: The 1849 gold rush.

5. *peltries*: This should be pelties, animal skins.

6. *Poncho*: Here the name of Lucy's mustang, but also a Latin American cloak with a hole for the head.

7. *St Louis*: Missouri's biggest city.

CHAPTER 3
John Ferrier Talks With the Prophet

1. *the Danite Band, or the Avenging Angels*: The Danites took their name from Dan, son of Jacob, one of the founding tribes of Israel. They were expelled by Joseph Smith.

2. *Gentile*: i. e. non-Mormon.

3. *We Elders have many heifers*: Heber C. Kemball, who took over from Brigham Young, regularly called his wives cows in his sermons.

CHAPTER 4
A Flight for Life

1. *You shall smart for this*: 'He that is surety for a stranger shall smart for it', Proverbs 11:15.

2. *Carson City*: A non-Mormon city in Nevada near the border with California, founded in 1858 by Christopher Carson.

CHAPTER 6
A Continuation of the Reminiscences of John Watson MD

1. *I got it from over-exposure and under-feeding*: It is more likely that an aortic aneurism at that time would have been a consequence of syphilis.

2. *York College*: The medical college at New York University.

3. *I went round suspecting no harm*: Having had his suspicions aroused by an advertisement to collect a ring and having taken suitable precautions, why was Hope not suspicious of being asked, *by name*, to return to the same house with his cab?

CHAPTER 7
The Conclusion

1. *growler*: Four-wheeled cab.

2. *brougham*: Closed, four-wheeled vehicle named after Henry, Lord Brougham (1778–1868), lawyer and statesman.

3. *jarveys*: Cockney slang for coachmen and a corruption of Gervase, St Gervase having the emblem of a whip.

4. Populus me sibilat, at mihi plaudo

  Ipse domi simul ac nummos contemplar in arca:

'The public hiss at me, but I'm pleased with myself at home when I look at the money in my strongbox', Horace, *First Satire*, lines 66–7. It refers to a rich man in Athens.